The Sh

As Theo lay i
with question
legend, the laughter on the moors, the
pendant, and finally Aron. Why had he
avoided her? And how had he left the
alley? . . . A sound began to echo in her
ear. Shhh . . . shhh . . . it lulled her, like a
whisper on the wind . . . Shhh . . .
Shoshawna.

OTTO COONTZ

The Shapeshifters

A Magnet Book

The lines on p 86 are reprinted by permission
of the publishers and the Trustees of Amherst College
from *The Poems of Emily Dickinson*, edited by
Thomas H. Johnson (Cambridge, Mass.:
The Belknap Press of Harvard University Press),
copyright 1951, © 1955, 1979
by the President and Fellows of Harvard College.

First published in Great Britain in 1987
by Methuen Children's Books Ltd
This Methuen Teens paperback edition first published 1988
by Methuen Children's Books
A Division of OPG Services Ltd
Michelin House, 81 Fulham Road, London SW3 6RB
© 1983 Otto Coontz
Printed in Great Britain by
Cox & Wyman Ltd, Reading

ISBN 0 416 10262 X

For my nephews Kris and Thad,
and my cousins Kim and Amy

Although some actual elements from Native American mythology appear in this book, the mythology I have attributed to the four Nantucket tribes is essentially my own invention and should not be taken as fact. I have also credited Nantucket with institutions that are of my own construction, and the island as it is described in this book should not be taken for the island as it actually exists at this writing.

Special thanks are due to the very special people listed below:

Justin O'Connor — who introduced me to the island. Sonny Booker and Paul Poor — my generous hosts. Karen Erickson, Stephen Pelton, and particularly, Lyn Hoopes — without whom, quite truthfully, this book would not have been written.

OTTO COONTZ 1983

Contents

The Shapeshifters

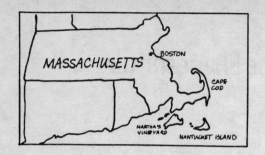

NANTUCKET ISLAND, MASSACHUSETTS

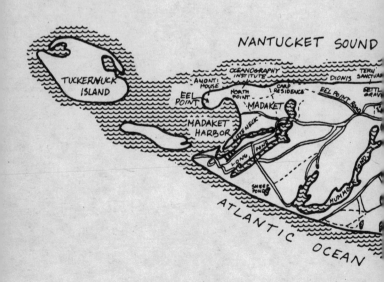

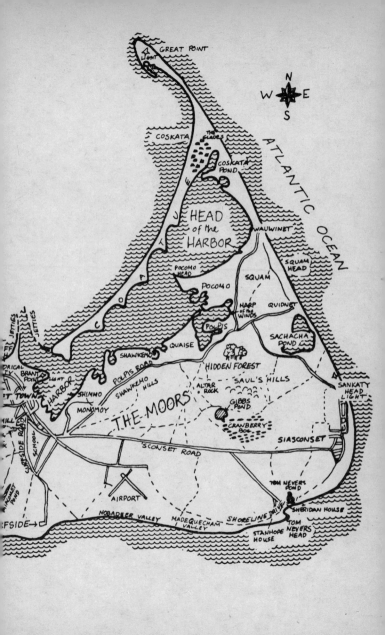

1 Destiny

"There she is, coming up on our right!" the pilot shouted above the drone of the small plane's engine. Theo Benedict leaned forward in her seat to peer out the oval window. Through the wispy clouds below, she spotted a tiny wedge of land. It looked a bit like a boomerang drawn in green and yellow crayon, cut out and set adrift in the sparkling sea. For a moment she felt an odd, sinking feeling, like the pull of an undertow. Then the plane passed down through a heavy bank of clouds and the feeling passed.

"Theda, sit back." Her stepmother frowned, shifting in the seat beside her. "You've been fidgeting ever since we took off. Why don't you read your book?"

Theo shrugged, dutifully sat back in her seat, and stared up at the cockpit. It was hard putting up with the nagging and fussing, but she knew they wouldn't even be going to Nantucket if it weren't for Vicky. Her stepmother sighed, pressing a thumb and forefinger against the space between her eyes.

"Vicky? Are you all right?" Theo's father leaned forward from the seat behind and squeezed his wife's shoulder.

"I think I'm getting one of my migraines."

"It's the noise. This plane is positively primitive."

Theo's stepmother pushed on her dark glasses and

leaned her head back against the seat. Mr. Benedict motioned for Theo to move into the row behind. He hoped this vacation would help ease the tension between Vicky and Theo. He hoped, but Vicky's headache was not a good sign.

"Here, you can have the window." He gave Theo his seat and took one on the aisle. "Doesn't look like much for an island fifteen miles long, especially when you consider we've just flown twice that distance from the mainland." He gestured toward the window at the speck of land growing below. "The brochure says that Indians once lived here, till one of the colonial governors sold the island to settlers for thirty pounds and a couple of beaver hats. Pretty cheap, when you think that two hundred years later it became the whaling center of the world."

"When did they stop hunting whales?" Theo's face was still pressed to the window.

"About a hundred years ago. There's still a small, year-round community of fishermen living down there, but the big catch now is tourists." Mr. Benedict glanced over Theo's mop of dark curls at the island below. He could just make out the tiny white flecks of sailboats in the harbor.

"It looks different," Theo remarked thoughtfully, squinting down as the plane lost altitude.

"What do you mean?" her father asked, grinning. "Theo, we've never been here before."

"I must have seen a picture of it somewhere. An old one. Before they had all those buildings." But as she thought about it, Theo couldn't remember where. The plane banked to one side as it began to circle. Theo felt a strange tug, almost, she thought, as though the island were a powerful magnet drawing them down.

Seems an unlikely place for a *Destiny Jones* fan club to spring up, she mused. It was too beautiful, too wild, too far out to sea. Theo could not imagine anyone here glued to a television screen every afternoon, even if her father did write the *Destiny* scripts and her stepmother played the lead role. But the invitation had come, and Vicky had grudgingly agreed. They were getting a house on the beach for three full weeks, Theo thought with excitement, and just because a handful of fans on the island wanted to meet Vicky DeVane. Being related to a celebrity definitely had its advantages. Already, Theo was imagining running over the sand and into the sparkling surf below.

As the plane glided over grass-covered cliffs and on toward the harbor, Theo caught sight of a lighthouse pointing up at them like a finger. I *have* seen this before, she thought, studying the scene below — the jetties, the harbor and marshes, and, off in the distance, the moors. The island was famous, she reminded herself; she *must* have seen pictures somewhere. As she caught sight of a church spire poking up through the green, a faint, dull beating began to sound in her ears. Then the plane dipped lower. It was like a distant heartbeat and seemed to come from below, almost, she thought, as though the island were some huge living thing.

"My ears just popped," her father remarked, looking down at his watch. Barely one o'clock. The little plane had made good time.

Theo pressed her fingers to her ears, trying to stop the odd pulsing sound, but it only grew louder. This wasn't just from the altitude drop, she thought, about to say something to her father. But then her ears cleared as well, and abruptly the throbbing sound stopped.

"The three ships from the Boston Tea Party once moored at the end of that wharf!" the pilot shouted back. "And that's Main Street just below us! Still has the original cobblestones!"

As the plane began to level off, Theo took one more long, sweeping glance, picking out a solitary windmill on a hill high above the town. Its sails jerking in their locks, straining to spin, made her feel strangely uneasy. It looked ancient and unused, with its gray, weather-beaten shingles and its one broken window looking over the town like a cold, unblinking eye. Catching the glint of sun on its broken shards, Theo had the peculiar feeling that it watched her. But that's nonsense, she told herself, pushing the feeling away as the plane glided past.

Below the hill, she spotted a low brick building that appeared to be a school. Watching the students scurrying over the athletic field like ants, Theo gloated. Her junior high in Manhattan had already closed for the summer. Turning in her seat to get a better look, her feet swung up against the bottom of Vicky's chair. Vicky tilted her head to the crack between the seats and scowled behind her glasses.

"Would you calm down?" she grumbled. "Will, would you make her sit still?"

Anger flickered in the back of Theo's mind. Like an electric current, it tingled down her spine. Please don't let Vicky spoil things again, she wished fervently to herself. The tingling rippled out of her like a wave. It was an odd sensation, not quite like anything she'd felt before. Been sitting too long, she thought to herself, eager to stretch her legs and get on solid ground. Leaning back, she fastened her safety belt, waiting for the ground to thump up from below.

The plane rocked violently and abruptly angled up again.

"Slight downwind, nothing to worry about!" the pilot shouted back.

In the schoolyard below, Theo spotted a boy with his arms upstretched. Not waving, exactly, she thought. It looked almost as though he was reaching.

2 A Tremor of Recognition

Aron Amonti's hands were raised to the sky, but his face was contorted, as if not a baseball but the moon itself were hurtling down.

"Go for it!" the boy on the pitcher's mound shouted.

The base runner was rounding third and heading for home when the ball hit the ground with a dull thud no more than a yard from Aron's feet. His eyes were still glued to the sky, following the path of a small plane dipping behind the trees in its descent to the island's airport. For a fraction of a second there was an odd, barely perceptible buzz in the air, like the sound of an angry fly. Aron tilted his head to one side, listening. No one else seemed to have heard it.

"It was a piece of cake!" the pitcher griped, slamming his glove to the ground. "You didn't even try!"

"Sheridan!" the coach cried out impatiently, "it's only a game! Calm down! Amonti, throw the ball!"

Distracted, Aron lobbed the ball four yards short of the pitcher's mound.

"Thanks for the effort!" Kip Sheridan called out sarcastically, striding toward the ball.

"Sheridan, take the bench!" the coach barked.

"The bench! What for?" Kip cried back indignantly.

"To give yourself some time to think about team etiquette!" the coach replied sternly. "Miller, take the pitcher's mound!"

"Team etiquette? Since when is he worried about etiquette? What does he think we're playing, croquet?" Kip muttered as he stalked past Miller to the bench. Why didn't the coach chew out Amonti? he wondered. Cripes, it usually drives him bananas when guys doze in the field. Kip slouched on the bench and stared at Amonti moving back to the outfield. His angular body and long, fluid strides gave him the look, Kip thought, of a cobra weaving through the grass. Aron took his position, brushed the dark hair back from his eyes, and glanced briefly in the direction of the airport.

The game continued. Kip brooded as he watched.

Amonti had never played so lousy in his life. What was the matter with the kid? Kip wondered. He was one of the best players in the seventh grade, but today it was as though he wasn't even there. And what was it with the coach today? The banter was all part of the game. He'd never benched anyone for it before.

When the game was over, the coach herded the boys back into the locker room. Amonti followed the coach into his office while the others undressed. Maybe the kid was feeling sick, Kip thought as he headed down to the showers.

". . . and you're feeling it now?" He overheard the coach as he passed the office door. He saw Aron nod. "Better go down and tell Michael Hogarth. It's half an hour earl——" The coach cut himself off, having spotted Kip outside the doorway. "What are you gawking at? Hit the showers, Sheridan."

Guess Aron *was* feeling bad, if he was getting sent down to the principal. Kip hung up his towel and stepped into the showers, beginning to feel a bit guilty. He closed his eyes as the hot spray beat against his shoulders. If Aron was sick, he ought to apologize, he decided, peering through the steam at the ghostly shapes of the other boys. Funny, Kip thought, not so much joking around in here as usual. Guess the coach's mood got everyone uptight.

"Move it, boys." The coach stuck his head in the doorway. "Next period starts in eight minutes."

Kip headed back out to the lockers. As he sat down on the bench he noticed Aron's locker, already empty. Or nearly. Something black and glistening on the floor of the locker caught Kip's eye. Sliding down the bench, he picked it up. It resembled a large thumbnail, only more delicate. A few others just like it were scattered under the bench. If they hadn't been so big, he'd have guessed they were fish scales.

"Sheridan, get with it! You only have five minutes!" The coach stood at the door of his office watching him.

Kip quickly dressed, crammed his gym suit into his book bag, and pushed through the locker-room doors.

When the next class began, he noticed that Aron's seat was empty.

Norma Pocket glanced in her rearview mirror at the family in the back of her cab. The woman leaned toward one window, her face hidden behind dark glasses and a floppy broad-brimmed hat. Across from her, a lean handsome man stared pensively straight ahead. Between them sat Theo, craning her neck, trying to catch a glimpse of the meadows rushing by.

Up ahead, at the side of the road, stood a large red sign with the word MARENACK printed boldly across it.

"What's Marenack?" Theo asked the cabbie, having counted four of the signs since they left the airport.

"An off-island developer," Norma Pocket answered with an edge of disapproval in her voice. "This past year the Marenack Corporation's been buying up land all over the island. Resorts are going to go up wherever you see those signs. Won't recognize the island once the project's under way."

Theo looked past her father, out to the open fields. The tall, golden grass rippled in the wind. And the sky,

Theo thought to herself, she'd never *seen* so much sky. Looking out at this view, breathing in the salt air, Theo understood why the driver wouldn't want buildings here. A few hundred yards along, she spotted another Marenack sign by a pond where sheep were grazing. Theo leaned forward in her seat to ask about it.

"Theda, sit still," Vicky snapped before Theo could open her mouth. Theo sank back in her seat and leaned her head against her father's shoulder. Norma shifted gears and turned the cab down the shoreline drive.

"The sand's bone white," Mr. Benedict remarked. "Almost looks like snow."

Theo sat forward again. "Are we going to be right on it?" she asked the driver.

"Theda," Vicky interrupted, "stop pestering the driver."

"It's all right. She's no bother." Norma flashed back a split-second smile. "You can step out your back door right into the water."

"How's the swimming? Is it cold?" Theo, her arms dangling over the front seat, peered ahead at a white sail bobbing on the horizon.

"Not too cold. But you have to watch the undertow."

The cab passed several gray-shingled houses nestled in the dunes. Everywhere, unruly patches of beach grass fluttered in the offshore breeze. Suddenly, Theo saw dozens of small gray and white birds shooting up from the grass.

"What are they? Baby gulls?" One darted toward the windshield, gave a high shrill cry, then flew away.

"They're terns," Norma answered. "They nest in the dune grass."

"On the ground?" Theo's brows pulled together. A few more terns swooped toward the car. "What if a cat came along?"

Norma laughed. "Don't worry. Nature made sure they could take care of themselves. We also call them bullet beaks. Any cat who wanders down here is going to regret it."

Theo caught Norma's eye in the mirror. The woman was smiling at her, a warm, generous smile that reminded Theo of her mother's.

"Would you roll up the windows? My hair's getting mussed." Vicky pulled the brim of her hat down against the breeze. Mr. Benedict put up his window, but Norma left the front ones open, seemingly ignoring the request.

The cab took a sharp curve, and for a moment it seemed to Theo that they were going to drive right out onto the beach. Then they turned in between two high dunes topped with a picket fence. On the other side sprawled a house as long as a ship. A flag flapped from a mast sticking up from one end of an open deck. A few yards beyond this, the surf was breaking.

"Wow!" Theo exclaimed, now leaning halfway into the front of the cab.

"You're kidding." Her father's voice came from behind her. "We'll be lost in it."

"You don't like it?" Norma asked. "It's the nicest place on Tom Nevers Head."

"It's marvelous. It's just that I expected something more like a cottage." Mr. Benedict reached across the seat for Vicky's hand. She pulled it away, still glaring out the window.

The cab came to a stop and Theo scrambled out. She took the stairs up the deck two at a time, then ran back down to the edge of the water and kicked off her shoes.

"It's great!" she shouted, wading a ways out into the foam.

Her father smiled and waved, then unloaded the trunk and helped Norma carry the bags. Theo frowned when she saw Vicky glancing sullenly over the dunes. Please don't let her spoil it, she thought. Please.

"Would you look at this piano!" Mr. Benedict exclaimed. "Who owns this place, Liberace?"

Norma grinned as she set down the bags. "Some people named Stanhope. It cost them so much to build it, they have to rent it to pay off the mortgage."

"Will, could I see you in here for a moment?" Vicky stood by an open door off the hall.

"Would you excuse me for a minute?" Mr. Benedict looked apologetically at Norma.

"I have to be getting back anyway." Norma started for the door.

"Hold on." Theo's father pulled out his wallet. "What do I owe you for the cab?"

"It was taken care of at the other end." Norma smiled warmly as she retreated. "Enjoy your stay."

"Bye!" Theo called after her, dropping her shoes by the steps to the deck.

"There aren't many cabbies on the island," Norma said with a wink. "I'm sure you'll see me again."

"I hope so." Theo smiled back, feeling drawn to that broad, tan face with its laugh lines etched about the eyes. *That's* it, Theo thought, it's those soft gray eyes. They *were* just like her mother's.

"Will . . ." Vicky sighed impatiently as the front door closed. Theo watched her father shuffle across the shag rug and follow Vicky into the hall. Sometimes he reminded her of a sad little puppy who never gets petted, just scolded.

"Why did they stick us out in the middle of nowhere?" Vicky began. "What are we supposed to do with ourselves? If I'd known we were going to Siberia . . ." Then the door closed, muffling her angry voice. She's trying to ruin it, Theo thought miserably, feeling her face grow hot as the anger flickered in the back of her mind. Listening to Vicky's grumbling drift down the hall, Theo saw the light from the deck doors fade as a cloud passed overhead. Out of the corner of her eye, she glimpsed a single black feather flutter across the rug and come to rest against the doorsill. As she crossed to pick it up, still brooding, the room grew darker. Above her, a small chandelier began to sway, its tiny crystals tinkling like breaking glass. When she reached for the feather, a hushed roar sounded in her ears. Was it the sea? she wondered. The feather felt wet. Then she saw a thin sheet of water seeping in under the door, and, looking up, she suddenly faced a solid wall of water where the sky had been. Something long and thin, like an eel, slithered by the top of the door. The roaring grew louder.

"Stop it!" she screamed. "Make it stop!"

"Theo?" Mr. Benedict stepped out to the hall. His daughter stood in a shaft of sunlight slanting through the glass doors. Her hands were pressed to her ears and her eyes were shut. She was trembling.

"Theo." He crossed the room and squeezed her shoulder. Theo shuddered, dropping her arms to her sides. She squinted at the sun pouring though the deck doors, then out at the glistening sand and the sparkling sea beyond. The shadow of a cloud slid over the beach and into the pounding surf.

"Are you all right?" Her father turned her chin upward. The bright sun made her blink a tear from her eye. She nodded. For that flash of a second it had all seemed so real. The water, the roaring; what had it been?

"You're sure?" Her father brushed a hand through her curls.

"I'm O.K.," she answered, but still she felt shaken. Could it have been an optical illusion? she wondered, staring out at the cloud's reflection gliding over the water.

"It's stuffy in here." Mr. Benedict pulled open the doors and stepped out onto the deck. It's these fights with Vicky, he thought to himself, wishing there was something he could do to make it less hard on Theo.

Theo watched the feather flutter out the door and across the deck. The wind picked it up and carried it down to the shore. Walking out past her father, she glimpsed something gray and gnarled with sticklike arms splashing in the surf.

"Dad!" Theo pointed. "What is it?"

"What?" he asked, his eyes following her outstretched finger; but the thing had vanished beneath the water.

"Guess it was just an old tree stump," Theo mumbled. "For a minute, it looked like it was alive."

"It probably got dragged down in that undertow Norma Pocket was talking about. If you want to go swimming, let me know so I can keep an eye out."

"I'm not so sure I want to, now, with that undertow and creepy old stumps in the water."

"You'll want to if it stays this hot. I'll tell you what. After we unpack, we'll look for a good place to swim."

Theo was staring down at a long winding track in the sand. Why hadn't she seen it before, she wondered, when she'd first run across the beach? It looked almost as if a wide hose had been dragged in a swirling pattern from beneath the deck and then alongside the house. In the hollow of the track, she spotted several glistening black shapes. They'd be hard to miss, she thought to herself, yet her footprints passed right by them.

"Mind if I walk around a little, Dad, before I go in to unpack?"

"'Course not. Go ahead." Her father started inside.

Theo walked down from the deck and stooped by the track. These black things are weird, she thought, sort of like shells, but soft. She stuck one in her pocket and followed the track down the beach.

A little way from the house, the winding trail turned up toward the dunes. More and more of the funny shells were scattered in the track. They crunched beneath her feet as she began to trudge up the embankment. Hearing voices on the other side, she crouched in the grass at the top.

Below her, Theo saw Norma Pocket's cab pulled to the side of the shoreline drive. She was calling to a boy pushing a bicycle out of a grassy ditch. Is that what made the track? Theo wondered. But it seemed a bit wide for a bike tire, and she hadn't noticed any footprints. Theo watched the boy wheel the bike up to the cab.

"It's her." His voice, edged with excitement, carried faintly up the hollow between the dunes. Was he talking about Vicky? Theo wondered. Was he one of Vicky's fans? Perhaps he'd been hiding beneath the deck to get a look at her, she thought with amusement. Well, it wouldn't be the first time someone did something like that. Theo turned and slid back down the dune to the beach.

After Theo had left to wander along the shore, a tall gaunt woman came from a valley between the dunes and joined Norma and the boy.

"Where's Hogarth?" Norma asked.

"He still hasn't shed the form," Adele Pocket replied. "He's watching."

"And the test?"

"It's she, but her power is weak," the woman answered.

"But she did stir each of the elements," the boy put in.

"Only slightly. And it came from her anger," the

gaunt woman corrected. "Or fear. I heard her parents argue. Although these disturbances come from her, she is far, still, from controlling them. But we don't want any accidents, so we'll have to watch closely while she is awakening. As her power builds, we might set her a trial or two, direct her a bit."

"And the vision?" Norma asked. "Does she have the vision, too?"

"Yes, so we must be careful. We must help her toward her past without opening the future."

"But if she has the vision . . ."

"She will not understand the visions, and we'll block them when we can. Tomorrow she'll have the shaping stone. The depth of her mark on the pendant will tell us when she's ready."

"Will she be ready by solstice?" the boy asked.

"By solstice, or sooner," the gaunt woman answered. "Aron, you better get back to school." She climbed into the seat beside Norma.

"Will I see you at the Circle?" He straddled his bike.

"No," the woman answered. "I must clear the well in the forest. But Norma will be there to stand in the place of Wind." Then the cab containing the Pocket sisters sped past him down the shoreline drive.

3 Things Felt but Not Yet Seen

Further down the beach, in a modest gray shingle house, Kip Sheridan's mother was tacking down a square of loose linoleum by the kitchen counter. She looked up from the floor as the screen door was pushed open.

"George? You're back early," she mumbled through the tacks in her mouth. Mr. Sheridan opened the refrigerator door and pulled out a beer. He flipped off the cap and drank thirstily.

"Another tile come up?" He sank into a seat by the kitchen table.

"Third this week." Mrs. Sheridan banged a tack into a corner of the tile. The house was old and badly in need of repair.

"George? Is something wrong?"

"Huh?" He was peeling the bottle label with meticulous concentration, the sort of thing he did when something weighed on his mind.

"What's the matter? You seem awfully quiet." Mrs. Sheridan straightened up and nudged the replaced tile with her foot.

"The seismograph at the oceanography station acted up today. But I'm not too sure what to make of it. Probably nothing to worry about."

"If you don't think it was anything to worry about, then why are you worried?"

"Jinny, I'm not worried. I'm confused."

"All right, confused then." Mrs. Sheridan poured herself a cup of coffee and took a seat across from him. "So, what does it mean, this thing with the seismograph?"

"You know how the instrument works. It measures any movement in the earth's crust. When two plates along a fault line shift, they send out vibrations, or tremors. The machine picked up some activity a little before one today." Mr. Sheridan frowned. "But the only reason we have a seismograph on the island is to help measure the Newbury Fault. That runs from Newbury on up through Portland, Maine. There are no faults around here, at least none that we know of. This whole area was monitored and mapped out years ago."

"Is that what this was, a tremor along the Newbury Fault?" Mrs. Sheridan shifted in her seat.

"No. I checked with the mainland seismograph stations. There wasn't a peep from any of them. Our station was the only one to pick anything up."

"Then what do you think it was?"

Mr. Sheridan said nothing.

"George, was it near the island?"

"Now, I don't want you to start worrying about it. The vibration was so weak it barely registered, no more than a nick in the graph, well under a two. That wouldn't even be enough to feel. For all we know, it might just be a bug in the graph. The equipment's old. Might have loosened up in the bedrock over the years. I have someone checking it over. Ought to know if it's a bug before dinner."

"And if it isn't?"

He looked up. "Then we'll take a plane up to measure any abnormalities in the gravitational pull over the island. Just to be on the safe side. But I'll bet you a dinner at the Gone-Fish-Inn it's a bug in the graph."

"Just tell me we're not sitting on a fault, and I'll take *you.*" Mrs. Sheridan grinned, but he could see she was uneasy.

"You're on." Mr. Sheridan started for the door.

"Where are you going?"

"Harry Carp gave me some blues and haddock. They're in the pickup. I just stopped by to drop them off before heading back to the station."

Walking back along the shore to the Stanhope house, Theo had the peculiar feeling that she was being watched. Glancing back at the dunes and the beach stretching out behind her, she saw no one. The incoming tide washed over her feet, and she turned to look out at the breakers. The sea seemed increasingly restless. The whitecaps whipped in toward the beach and broke against the shore. But the wind, she noticed, was peculiarly calm.

When the water ran back down the shore, it left strands of white foam all around her, like skeleton fingers clawing up from the sand. Again Theo had the odd sensation that someone, or something, was watching. She stared into the hollow of the next wave curling toward the shore. The water was murky and green with the shadows of things churning in the undertow. For an instant she thought she saw something gray, like a face but not quite human. An enormous face with eyes on the ends of sticks, and gnarled, crooked arms stretching out . . . the stump, she remembered, but before she could look any closer the breaker crashed to the shore, spitting out jellyfish, shells, and seaweed. Seaweed snakes, Theo thought to herself, watching the kelp and driftwood in the water tumble and writhe. Shadows that look like waves, seaweed snakes, and stumps with eyes and arms.

"Theo," she said to herself, "you've got to stop seeing things." Why couldn't she relax? she wondered. Why couldn't she just enjoy the cool water and the warm sand between her toes? What was it that was making it all so frightful? Why was she so on edge? Theo started back to the house. Beneath the breakers behind her, something gray crawled deeper in the water and again the sea grew calm.

When the bell for the last class rang, the room grew silent as abruptly as though someone had pulled a plug. Miss Feldspar, the English teacher, crossed to her desk and picked up a stack of papers. Aron Amonti's seat, Kip noted, was still empty.

"Let's not waste any time." Miss Feldspar's hands shook slightly as she dropped the worksheets on the five front desks. "Please pass them back face down." The teacher walked to the front of the room and leaned against her desk. She seemed unusually anxious, Kip thought as he watched her glance repeatedly from the clock to the door.

"The first part is made up of twenty multiple-choice questions that require no more than memory. However, the essay question at the bot——" She cut herself off. Aron Amonti came through the door and quickly took his seat by the window.

"The essay question at the bottom of the page is designed to make you think. You'll have forty minutes." Miss Feldspar glanced up at the clock. "All right. Begin."

Kip watched Miss Feldspar pace nervously at the front of the room. She was staring at Aron. Why hadn't she said anything when the boy walked in late? Funny that he walked in at all, after missing the last class altogether, Kip thought. He peered at Aron, who was hunched over his desk, pencil rapidly jotting on the worksheet. Speedy recovery, Kip thought to himself.

"Sheridan, you'd better begin." Miss Feldspar started up the aisle. Kip dropped his eyes to the paper on his desk.

Twenty minutes later, a light knock sounded at the classroom door. Glancing up, Kip spotted Mr. Hogarth, the principal, beckoning Miss Feldspar out to the hall. The man's black hair was plastered to his skull as if he'd just taken a shower. Miss Feldspar seemed even more anxious now than before. What's with her? Kip wondered. From his seat by the door, he could hear them talking in hushed tones.

"We're sure now. It's her, she's come home," Mr. Hogarth whispered as she closed the door. The sound of scribbling pencils filled the enormous stillness of the classroom. *Who's* come home? Kip wondered. Then, looking at the clock, he turned back to the test.

"Hey, Aron!" Kip called to the boy at the bike rack. "Sorry if I was kind of hard on you during the game," he apologized as he walked up to him. He didn't know the boy very well. Aron always seemed a bit shy, in his own world. "What's the matter, were you feeling sick or something?"

"I'm all right," Aron mumbled, fumbling with the chain, seeming slightly shaken by the intrusion.

"How'd you make out on the test?" Kip asked, trying to break the ice.

"O.K." Aron dropped the bike chain in his basket and kicked up the kickstand.

"You notice how nervous Feldspar was? You'd think *she* had to take the exam. That essay question was a killer."

"I have to go." Aron cut him off, straddling his bike and pushing away.

Weird, Kip thought, watching Aron glide out of the driveway. That guy is *weird!*

4 The Call of the Moors

Coasting down Atlantic Avenue, Kip could not shake Aron from his mind. There was something strange about him that Kip couldn't quite figure. He was bright enough, and a decent athlete, but he was always so distant, holding himself apart.

Starting up the hill, Kip pedaled harder. As the sea came into view in the distance, his thoughts turned to summer vacation. Just one more week, then freedom, he thought to himself, looking forward to long days fishing on his father's boat. It was good out in the boat, away from all the tourists. Already they were beginning to arrive like locusts, crammed onto the ferries. In his mind he pictured the crowds that would swarm through the town. He imagined the bodies jammed together on the beaches, and how the breezes would be filled with the smoke of cookouts and the sound of blaring radios. And everywhere, Kip thought, there would be litter; on beaches, in the meadows, drifting in the harbor.

Over the years, the front of the island had been built up by the expanding tourist industry, and this growth, many islanders feared, was spreading like a cancer toward the inland and quiet back shores. Still, there were parts of the island Kip knew no tourists were likely to find: quiet places, like the moors with their hidden glades and ponds.

Riding on, Kip spotted a Marenack sign at the edge of a field of daisies. Someone else, he thought with disdain, had sold out to the off-island developer. It was bad enough that Marenack's projects were springing up all over town, but way out here was uncomfortably close to the moors.

The ocean breeze fluttered Kip's collar and played in his hair as he coasted down the road. Already pinpoint freckles were scattered over his face and arms, and his skin held the pink glow of a burn. He pushed on his brakes and turned down a dirt road that led into the moors. This region of the island was uninhabited, rugged land covered with low brush and hidden bogs.

The bike rattled over the bumpy road, past low undulating hills cloaked with heather. Kip came to a great slab of stone known as Altar Rock, and stopped. This was his favorite place on the island, far enough away from the rest of the world to exist in a time of its own. All around, the moors were just as they'd been when Indians lived on the island.

Climbing to the top, Kip knelt by a series of grooves cut into the rock. They formed an arrow with sweeping, winglike arms stretching out from its base. The popular story was that the carving had been made over three hundred years before by one of the island tribes. But little was known of the Nantucket tribes, and apart from this symbol and the occasional discovery of an arrowhead, little remained.

Kip stretched out on the warm stone and squinted at the clear blue sky. The air hummed with the call of crickets and the peepers in the bog. They lulled him like a lullaby. Kip closed his eyes and dozed in the heat of the sun.

Driving home for supper, Kip's father saw a couple of dozen cars parked in front of the Amonti house. Funny, he thought, that they would have such a large party and he wouldn't have heard about it. Looking over the cars, he saw that Norma Pocket was there, along with Dr. Perry, Mr. Hogarth, and some of Kip's teachers. He passed the pickups of several fishermen he knew, then spotted Harry Carp's, parked at the edge of the yard. Harry's five-year-old daughter Terry waved from the back of the truck. Mr. Sheridan slowed to a stop.

"Hi, Terry. What's going on?" he called out to the child.

"Daddy and Mommy are at the Amontis'. I have to stay with Sandy while they talk." The child had one arm wrapped around the Carps' retriever.

"What are they talking about?"

The girl hugged the dog tighter and only smiled shyly.

"Did something bad happen?" Mr. Sheridan asked.

"Not *bad*," Terry answered, as though the man should know better. "Later, there's going to be a party. And me and Sandy can go in then, too," she added importantly.

"Well, you have a good time, then." Mr. Sheridan winked at the girl and pulled away. Odd, he thought, that Harry hadn't mentioned anything about the Amontis having a party when he saw him earlier. Not that he minded, really, considering he didn't really know the family very well. As he picked up speed, his mind turned back to the seismograph.

At Altar Rock, Kip stirred in his sleep, his face hot with the burning rays of the sun. Suddenly a chilly wind coursed over him, followed by the sound of a deep-throated laugh. Startled awake, he sat up abruptly, listening to the sound echo over the moors. If there were anyone else in the hills, he thought, he should be able to see them. But all around he saw nothing but the scraggly shrubs and the glint of small ponds. Kip shrugged and started to his feet, then waved a hand at the sound of a fly near his head. Funny, he thought, the air now felt cold as ice against his skin. In the distance he spotted the sun hanging over the ocean, burning a deep orange in its descent. He'd been dozing a good deal longer than he'd thought. Climbing back onto his bike, he heard the odd laugh again, fainter. It seemed to come from Hidden Forest, a small woods concealed in a valley between the hills. The buzzing sounded again in his ear, but he could see nothing in the air. Then the buzz and the laughter abruptly broke off, and the moors fell silent. It was an odd laugh, Kip thought to himself as he coasted back down the road. It was unlike any laugh he'd heard before, more defiant than happy.

Behind him, a searing ray of sun grazed Altar Rock, casting a long shadow down the hill toward the wooded valley. On the longest day of the year, the shadow of Altar Rock would plunge to the heart of Hidden Forest.

Theo sat on the steps to the deck, hair dripping, a faint glow of sun on her shoulders. Grinning, she watched her father splash out of the water and sprint up the beach.

"You looked like a seal," she kidded. He was puffing and his face was flushed.

"Didn't realize how out of shape I was." He sat down to catch his breath, glancing back toward the open sea. "Isn't that something?" he said, then sighed with contentment. Together they watched the crimson-edged clouds gathering along the horizon.

"Those clouds almost look like a mountain of strawberry ice cream, they're so puffy and pink." Theo wriggled her toes in the sand, luxuriating in its silky warmth.

"Puffy and pink, like me." Her father squeezed a fistful of last winter's fat at his middle. "This has got to go." He frowned. "I spend too much time on my butt. Can't even remember the last time I went swimming." He pulled a towel off the railing and briskly rubbed it through his hair.

"Swimming?" Theo laughed and tossed a fistful of sand in his lap. "All we did was get pushed around by the waves. You call that swimming?"

"Current's too strong to do much more than wade," her father countered. "Maybe we can find a place where the water's calmer and the drop's not so sharp."

"Chicken," Theo teased him.

"Look who's talking!" Her father snapped the towel at her. "Every time a bit of seaweed floated by, you screamed bloody murder."

Theo blushed. "Only once, when that thing grabbed my foot."

"The monster from the deep," her father said with mock gravity, snaking his arms around her and tickling her till she writhed with laughter.

"All right! It was kelp! I give up! Stop it!"

"Would you two quiet down? I have a headache." Vicky stood at the door to the deck, frowning down at them.

"Sorry." Mr. Benedict craned his neck around. Vicky turned to go back in. "Oh, honey . . ." Theo's father called to stop her. "I was thinking of ordering a couple of pizzas for supper. Does that sound all right?''

"Get what you want. I'm not hungry.'' Vicky closed the door behind her.

"She doesn't like it here, does she?'' Theo asked in a low voice.

"She'll come around,'' Mr. Benedict said optimistically, brushing the sand from his feet and standing. "What are you going to do till supper?''

"I think I'll just sit out here for a while.'' Theo pulled her father's towel over her shoulders and dug her feet into the sand.

"Theo . . .'' Her father paused before starting up the stairs. "Don't worry about Vicky, O.K.? I just want you to have a good time.''

Theo smiled up at him. "I *am* having a good time.'' If only Vicky would relax, she thought, so her father could, too.

5 The Symbol on the Stone

Kip leaned his bike against the side of the house and started up the stairs. Flies buzzed against the screen as the back door swung shut behind him.

"Where were you?'' Mrs. Sheridan looked up from the kitchen table. "Dinner's been ready for an hour.''

"Fell asleep on the moors,'' Kip answered.

"Gram's out on the porch, Kip. Would you bring her in for dinner?''

Walking into the hall, Kip spotted his father through the open door of the den. He was pulling a large map of the island out of his briefcase.

"Hi, Dad."

"Hello, sport. How'd the English test go?"

"O.K. What are you doing with the map?"

"Just catching up on some work before dinner."

"George, supper's ready!" Kip's mother called out.

"I've gotta get Gram," Kip said as he continued down the hall. Stepping out to the porch, he found Gram rocking, her gaze on the waves breaking along the shore.

"Gram?" Kip touched the old woman's arm. She continued to rock, the ocean breeze fluttering thin white wisps of hair around her face. Lost in some secret thought, she was frowning, an odd little frown that crinkled across her brow.

The sun was buried behind red and violet streaks along the horizon. Fog was creeping in across the water.

"Man two," the old woman whispered.

"What, Gram?" Kip bent his ear to the old woman's lips, but now she was silent again, as though unaware that he was there.

Gram had lived on the island most of her life. When Kip was younger, she had told him many stories about the island's first colony, and how Nantucket had once been a great whaling port. She had worked in the library of the Historical Society and had known a lot about these things. Kip helped her up and led her into the kitchen.

At supper, Kip watched Gram methodically line up lima beans on the napkin by her plate. Even with the stroke, she still knew what she liked and didn't like. Before, she'd have simply left the beans on her plate, but since the stroke, she picked at her food like a child.

Kip looked up when his mother's voice rose with disappointment.

"Oh, George, I already told Evelyn we'd *be* there. Can't you take the day off? After all, it is the weekend."

"I can't, Jinny, I told you. Now the machine's checked out, we have to monitor the ground pull."

"Why can't it wait? You said yourself it probably wasn't serious." Mrs. Sheridan looked thoughtful for a moment. "This thing isn't serious, is it, George?"

"What thing?" Kip asked.

"George, is there more you're not telling me?"

"More about what?" Kip asked. "What's going on?"

"Nothing, sport. Just something to do with work."

"Can't they monitor the ground pull without you? I promised her we'd be there."

"I'm the only one with a background in seismology." He shrugged. "No one else knows how to do it."

"You *are* worried about it, aren't you?" Mrs. Sheridan stared hard at her husband. Kip's father was silent.

"Worried about what?" Kip persisted.

"Stop that!" his mother suddenly snapped, glaring at the row of beans lined up by his grandmother's plate. "If you're not going to eat them, just leave them."

Gram looked as though she'd been slapped. She tried to fold up the napkin, but her hands trembled so that the beans tumbled out and onto the floor.

"I wish you wouldn't shout at her," Kip's father intervened. "You know it makes her nervous."

"And my nerves are made of steel?" Mrs. Sheridan stooped to the floor and picked up the scattered beans. "One minute she's docile as a cat. The next, she's gallivanting up and down the beach in her nightgown." Kip could see the muscles in his mother's face grow tight. "Today, right after lunch, she disappeared again. I nearly lost my mind looking for her. Know where I found her? All the way up at Madequecham, just sitting there like a rock, with the tide streaming up all around her, mumbling 'man' or 'two' or some such nonsense. It's a full-time job just watching her."

"I know, dear, I'm sorry, I know." Mr. Sheridan spoke softly now, laying a hand on his wife's arm.

"Misplacing things, talking nonsense, disappearing." Kip's mother was close to tears. "And now this business about a fault . . ."

"Kip, take Gram out to the porch, would you?" his father said quietly.

What was it that set his mother off? Kip wondered as the door to the porch slammed behind them. He helped Gram into her chair, then leaned on the railing beside her. Looking down at her soft wrinkled face made him ache inside. He wondered if she'd heard. Since the stroke you could never tell just how much she caught. Gram was like the tide — sometimes in, sometimes out.

Kip remembered when it had happened. Gram had been working late at the Historical Society that night. When he and his father went to pick her up they'd found her slumped on the floor beside her desk. All around her, papers and books were strewn across the floor. It had terrified him.

After that, she was like a stranger, unable to talk, forgetting who people were and even where she was. It was as if her mind were a jigsaw puzzle that someone had clumsily scattered into a thousand disconnected pieces.

Gram was staring at a fat black beetle wandering drunkenly across the floor. It crept over the top of the stairs, then fell on its back on the step below. Its wiry legs wriggled mechanically in the air.

"Man two," Gram mumbled. Kip noticed one hand fidgeting in the pocket of her cardigan. He knelt beside her.

"What is it, Gram?"

But Gram only went on staring at the beetle trying to right itself. Kip gently tugged her hand from the pocket. Her clenched fist felt soft as tissue paper. As she watched the beetle flip over and straggle into a crack, Kip pried open her hand, uncoiling one bony finger after another. Nestled in her palm was a scrap of paper yellowed with age. Unfolding it, Kip saw that it was covered with odd markings in faded ink, markings that looked more like symbols than letters. In one corner were scrawled the numbers 6-21.

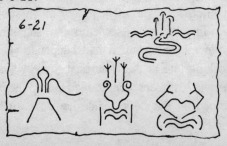

"What is it, Gram?" he repeated.

Gram just stared out over the water, a small sigh escaping her withered lips, as if some burden had been lifted from her mind. A crimson streak burned the horizon where the sun dipped beneath the sea. For a while Kip just sat on the stoop below her, turning the paper first one way then another, unable to make any sense of it. He stuck it in his pocket, drew his knees beneath his chin, and searched the darkening sky for the first star of night, so he could make a wish. His wish would be for Gram.

Later, on his way to bed, Kip passed by his parents' door.

"You sure you don't mind going alone?" he heard his father ask.

"It's all right, George. I'm used to it. Although I don't know what excuse to give Evelyn this time."

"Just say I had to work. You don't have to give her the details."

"I suppose," his mother sighed. "Would you turn down the bed while I talk to Kip?" She started from the room.

"Oh, there you are." She caught Kip outside the door. "Would you mind sticking around the house tomorrow afternoon, to keep an eye on Gram?"

"No, sure. I don't mind."

"Thanks, Kip. I'll be at Evelyn's from two to six if you need me." She ran her hand through his hair and smiled tiredly, then went down the hall to check on Gram.

"Dad?" Kip crossed the room.

"What's up?" His father sat down at the side of the bed and began to unlace his shoes.

"I know Gram's been a lot of trouble lately," Kip began.

"It'll be O.K." Mr. Sheridan smiled up at him. "Sometimes everything seems to pile up at once, and tonight poor Gram was the scapegoat."

"What do you mean?"

"Oh, when a whole lot of things are going wrong and one of them takes the blame for all the rest."

"What else was upsetting Mom?" Kip asked.

"Nothing to bother your head about. Don't worry, Mom's O.K."

At that moment Mrs. Sheridan came back in. "That walk this morning must have worn her out," she said. "She's already sound asleep. Time you were, too, Kip." She turned and hugged him goodnight.

Kip switched on the light by his bed and began to undress. Emptying his pockets, he pulled out Gram's slip of doodling. Examining it a second time, he noticed something familiar. He simply hadn't looked at it from the right angle before.

"That's *it*," he said with surprise. Now, seeing it right side up, he realized that it wasn't doodling at all, but something Gram must have dug up in her room, left over from her days at the Historical Society. What she was doing with this odd slip of paper now Kip couldn't guess, but he was certain the peculiar shapes represented old Indian symbols. At one side of the page was an exact copy of the symbol he'd seen earlier that day on Altar Rock — the arrow with the wings at the base.

Kip put the slip of paper on his desk, finished undressing, then crawled into bed and turned out the light. Out his window, farther up the shore, lights from the Stanhope house glowed dimly through the fog. He wondered who had rented the house this year. Too bad, he thought, whoever it was probably wouldn't have kids his age, not with another week of school left.

At the Stanhope house, Theo turned restlessly in her bed. From the other room she heard Vicky's muffled voice, still complaining. Vicky felt imprisoned in this house on the back island shore, and she'd harped on it all day. Theo felt sad for her father. She could tune Vicky out when she wanted, but for him there was no escape.

A breeze rustled the curtains at Theo's window, and as she turned to look out at the sky, she saw a large dark shape fluttering down behind the dunes. Hearing laughter from somewhere outside, she crept from her bed to the window. The figure of a woman, obscured by the darkness, emerged from the dunes. She paused at the top of a ridge a dozen yards from the Stanhope house, and for a long moment Theo felt as if the stranger was watching her. But then she moved on along the crest of the ridge, the wind rippling through her skirt.

It seemed late for a walk on the beach, Theo thought as she returned to her bed. Suddenly she realized she felt very drowsy. As she burrowed under the covers, drifting toward sleep, a picture began to form in her mind of the figure she'd seen from the airplane. Again it was reaching out to her, arms upstretched, alone on a grassy field. Drawn deeper into the vision, Theo felt pulled toward the boy, but suddenly the ground around him began to erupt, sprouting gray slabs of rock like ugly gravestones. Soon the clearing was covered with stones, stretching and rising higher, till a row of high buildings filled the place where the boy had been.

6 Meeting the Benedicts

Oatmeal dribbled down Gram's chin. Kip leaned from his seat and dabbed at it with a napkin. Gram never seemed aware of these things herself.

"Who took the Stanhope place?" he asked.

"Some New York people." Mrs. Sheridan was up on a chair hanging flypaper from the ceiling.

"Did you meet them?"

"No. I ran into Norma Pocket at Sunnyhurst.. She picked them up at the airport."

"What are they like? Did she say?" Kip asked.

"She thought they were Boat Basin. She said the mother was so buried under her hat and sunglasses that she couldn't even get a glimpse of her."

"The mother? Then there must be kids." Kip looked up with interest.

"One, about your age. Can't remember if she said a boy or a girl."

Suddenly the summer looked more promising. Kip stuck Gram's bowl on top of his and carried them to the sink. "Mom, I'm going to take a walk down the beach," he said.

"Could you put the garbage out first, Kip? These flies are driving me crazy." Mrs. Sheridan stepped down from the chair and looked up. Already a greenhead was buzzing frantically, trying to unstick itself from the paper spiral. Kip tied the top of the trash and dragged it out the door.

"And don't let any more flies in!" his mother called after him.

After dumping the rubbish in the bin, Kip started out over the dunes. Sand trickled into his sneakers as he plodded toward the Madequecham. About thirty yards down he passed the Stanhope house. Music drifted out from the open glass doors. Someone was playing the piano. Every summer since the Stanhopes had started renting, *some*one had played that piano. No one had ever played it very well, Kip thought, but whoever played it now was good. Not good, he amended, great! The music poured loudly over the dunes, powerful and rhythmic. Curious, Kip wandered up to the side of the house and peeked in the window.

An elegant woman in satin slacks paced across the shag carpet, hair the color of corn silk cascading over her shoulders.

"There was someone to meet us and drive us to the

house. What more do you want?'' A man's voice sounded from a part of the room Kip couldn't see. Kip surmised this was who was playing. The music continued to flow, rising in volume. Kip imagined powerful fingers rippling over the keys.

"Oh, come on, Will. It was rude not to have their whole group there to meet us,'' the woman complained in a husky voice, shaking her mane of blonde hair. Kip couldn't quite make out her face, which was hidden behind enormous sunglasses. Still, she looked a real knockout, he thought to himself. "It is customary, after all,'' she continued. "And it was rather déclassé to just dump us all in a cab. You'd think they'd have at least sent a limo.''

"This isn't New York, Vicky. I'd be surprised if they even had a limousine on the island. Look, perhaps they just thought you'd appreciate the privacy after the trip.'' The man's voice sailed over the music. Must be a pro, Kip decided, to be able to talk and keep playing like that.

"What time did she say that man would be here?'' The woman held up one hand and examined her nails.

"About one.'' The man played on.

The woman sulked. "I hate being cooped up in here.'' The satin made a swishing sound each time she passed the window.

"Why don't you *do* something?'' the man said impatiently.

"What?'' She stopped to jam a cigarette in a long silver holder.

"Why don't you go into town and take a look around? You could pick up some groceries."

"I'm not dressed for town, and my hair's a mess. What if someone recognized me? Oh, Will . . ."

"You look fine, Vicky." The man sighed. "Why can't you just relax? Lie out on the deck," he suggested.

"I can't. You know what the sun does to my skin."

"Then put on your sunscreen and wear a hat," the man grumbled, still not missing a chord.

"I hate slopping that stuff on. It's like bathing in Crisco." She turned toward the window. Kip ducked.

"Vicky, Vicky," the man's voice pleaded. "*What* do you want me to *do?*"

Kip peeked over the sill again. A man in a bathrobe had his arms around her. But the music was still going.

"Stop pounding at that piano!" the woman suddenly shouted.

"You told me to practice," a small voice rang out as the music plunked to a halt.

"You'll drive me crazy with that horrid piece."

"It's *not* horrid," the small voice protested. "It's the 'Grande Valse brilliante' by Chopin."

"Why don't you *valse* on down to the beach and build yourself a sand castle?" the woman remarked.

"Vicky," the man interrupted. "You know she has to practice."

"The same piece? Over and over and over?"

"I *have* to play it over and over until I get it right."

"I swear she plays that piece just to annoy me." The

woman frowned. "She's getting to be just like that horrible child in *The Bad Seed*."

"*The Bad Seed?*" the small voice asked. "Is that the old movie where the daughter drowns the boy who won the spelling bee?"

"And then she sets the caretaker on fire," the man finished. "Excellent script, excellent."

"And then the mother gives her sleeping pills," chimed the small voice. "Or does she shoot herself?"

"Doesn't the mother shoot the daughter?" The man stroked the stubble on his chin.

"I'd like to shoot both of you!" The woman tossed the cigarette holder out the window and stormed across the room.

"Where are you going?" the man asked.

"To call a cab. I'm going into town." A door slammed behind her.

"Wasn't she worried someone might recognize her?" the small voice asked.

"You know there's nothing Vicky likes more than signing a few autographs." The man sighed wearily. "Theo, I'm going to take a shower." A moment later another door closed and the piano music resumed.

Kip crouched over the cigarette holder glinting in the sun. Looks like real silver, he thought to himself. Probably worth some money. He picked it out of the sand and stuck it on the windowsill. The music stopped abruptly.

"Hey!" the small voice rang out. "What do you think you're doing?" A head of dark curls poked out the window.

Kip's face burned. "I . . . uh . . ."

"You were spying on us, weren't you?"

Kip shook his head from side to side.

"Admit it. You were spying on Vicky."

"I . . . I don't know who . . ."

"Admit it or I'll call my dad."

"Who's Vicky?" Kip asked nervously.

"Victoria DeVane!" The girl looked at him oddly. Kip stood there with a dumb expression.

"You mean you don't know Victoria DeVane?" The girl leaned out of the window, beaming. Kip shook his head.

"She's the star of *Destiny Jones*."

Kip was still shaking his head, stepping back from the window.

"Don't you ever watch TV?"

"We don't have one," Kip replied apologetically.

"You're kidding!" The girl seemed to find this amusing. Kip looked hurt. "I'm sorry. It's just that I'm surprised. I've never met anyone who didn't have a TV, and usually everyone I know pumps me for stories about Vicky. Some day I'm going to write a book. I already have the title. *Don't Call Me Mother: My Life with Vicky DeVane*. Dad said it could be a blockbuster."

"Blockbuster?" Kip repeated meekly.

"Sell millions. Say, do you really not know who Vicky is?" The girl regarded him closely.

"No." Kip shook his head one final time. "I'm sorry."

"Sorry!" The girl clapped her hands. "I think that's terrific! Theda Benedict. Theo, for short." Theo extended her hand. "Of course, you can't get much shorter than Theda," she added as Kip tentatively took her hand.

"I think Theda sounds like a missing tooth. It's after Theda Bara, you know."

"Who?"

"Some great silent-movie actress who died years and years ago. You go to movies much?"

"Uh-uh."

"Good." Theo climbed to the windowsill and jumped down beside him. Her T-shirt had MOVE OVER MOZART printed across the front.

"What's your name?"

"Kipper. Kip for short."

"Now *that's* a name. Does it mean anything?"

"Sort of." Kip began to blush again. "Kippers are little pieces of fish. Fillets of herring, I guess."

"How'd you get a name like that?"

"My granddad was a fisherman. He's the one who thought it up."

"Neat. I never met a fisherman." A car honked from the other side of the house, followed by the sound of a door banging closed. "You want to come in and look around? This place is like the Ritz."

Kip looked uncertain. Theo tugged him by the elbow.

"Come on, it's O.K." She led him around to the stairs and up the deck. "Vicky won't be back for a couple of hours. My playing always drives her out of the house."

"That was you?" Kip stopped in the doorway.

"Sure it was me. You play?"

"No."

"Too bad. It'd be neat to play a duet. That'd really drive Vicky up the wall."

"Is Vicky your sister?" Kip followed her into the living room.

"My sister?" Theo laughed. "She's my step-mother!"

"Then why do you call her Vicky?"

"She hates to be called mother. Says it makes her feel old. Like the title of my book. Didn't you get it?"

"Not really."

"That's O.K. Someday you'll read all about it."

"How come your last names are different?" Kip asked, sitting on the edge of a velvet couch, feeling terribly out of place.

"DeVane's the name she got famous with. Since that's the name everyone knew her by, she kept it when she married Dad." Theo sat down at the keyboard and plunked a few chords. "DeVane," she said thoughtfully. "Fits her better than Benedict, don't you think?" She played a few more chords, then spun around on the bench. "So, what's it like here? I've never been on an island before. Except for Staten Island. But that's just another big city."

Just then Theo's father stepped into the room, clean-shaven but still in his bathrobe.

"Thought I heard you talking to someone."

"Kip, meet my dad. Dad, this is Kip. Short for Kip-per, after herring fillet."

"Nice of you to drop by." Mr. Benedict shook Kip's hand. "I hoped Theo would meet someone her age."

"Can I invite him to lunch?" Theo asked, then turned to Kip. "Would you like to?"

"Hmm. Already?" Mr. Benedict said, glancing at his watch. "Why don't you two go ahead, Theo? I ought to try to do some work before Vicky comes back."

Theo led Kip out to the kitchen and started rummaging through the refrigerator. "Better cross your fingers," she said. "It's all junk Vicky brought from home. Mostly stuff you'd find in a cocktail lounge — smoked frogs' legs, caviar, stuff like that." Theo's voice echoed inside the refrigerator. "Hmm. This looks promising. Know what it is?" She held out a jar filled with something that looked like bits of aluminum floating in whipped cream. Kip shook his head. "Herring in cream sauce. In honor of you." She grinned. "Ever had it?"

"Nope."

"Me neither. Let's try it." Theo took two small plates from the cupboard and emptied half of the jar onto each. Together they sat at a small glass-topped table. Glimpsing his scruffy sneakers on the polished oak floor, Kip suddenly felt self-conscious. He pulled his feet under his chair.

Theo speared her fork into a metallic square of fish. "Well?" She held it suspended before her mouth. Kip did likewise. "Here goes."

After a moment, both of them grimaced. Theo swallowed and winced. Then she pushed her plate aside and said, "We could try the frogs' legs."

7 A Familiar View

Deciding to pass up lunch, Theo and Kip walked out onto the deck, where they found Theo's father brooding over his typewriter.

"We're going to take a look around, Dad."

"Fine, fine . . ." Mr. Benedict answered distractedly.

"Dad writes the scripts for *Destiny Jones*. He's working on one now," Theo explained. "All week," she whispered as they started down the stairs, "he's been stuck on this character named Rita."

"What's this show about?" Kip asked.

"Destiny's the name of this character Vicky plays, who keeps getting mixed up with all these different men. But every time she marries one, something goes wrong. Wrong for the man, but Destiny keeps getting richer from alimony settlements and inheritances. It's Destiny's destiny to be lucky in wealth and jinxed in romance. And the last man she fell for was already married to this Rita, see?"

Kip shook his head.

"Never mind. I'm sure you wouldn't want to watch it anyway," Theo concluded as she stepped onto the sand.

"I heard that, young lady," Mr. Benedict called gruffly from the porch, but when Kip glanced back over his shoulder he saw that her father was grinning.

Theo and Kip left their shoes at the foot of the steps and walked down to the shore. The water splashing over their feet was a welcome relief from the heat.

"Do you swim here much?" Theo asked.

"Sure, all the time." Kip picked up a stone and skipped it across the water.

"What about the undertow? Doesn't it scare you?" Theo stooped to examine a shell.

"Naw. There are plenty of sandbars along the back shore that break the tide. Look, you can see one up there." Kip pointed. "The undertow's only bad where the big drops are, like in front of your house. Just walk down the beach a little. You can tell where it's safe by the color of the water. Whenever the blue gets lighter you know there's a shelf."

Picking through bits of sea glass and broken shells beneath a tangle of seaweed, Theo remembered the odd black scales she'd found the day before. "Do you know what this comes from?" She pulled one out of her pocket.

Kip looked at it closely. It was just like the ones he'd found around Aron's locker. "Either some weird kind of shell or a scale off some very big fish. Where'd you find it?"

"In the sand around our house, and up in the dunes I saw lots more."

"Up in the dunes? Wonder how they got there." Handing it back, Kip also wondered again why they'd been around Aron's locker. The incoming tide swirled over his feet, leaving wreaths of froth around them. Theo waded in to her knees and tried skipping a rock. It bounced over three waves and disappeared.

"Hey, you're good." Kip grinned. The two of them strolled on down the beach, talking, trying to outdo each other's distance skipping rocks. Barely an hour had passed since Kip first met Theo, but already he felt he'd known her for years. It seemed, though, that she wasn't very happy, particularly when she talked about Vicky.

"Don't you like your mother?" Kip finally asked.

Theo had just picked up a stone and was aiming for an incoming wave.

"Stepmother," Theo corrected, flinging the stone. "Dad married Vicky a year ago. My real mom died when I was eight."

"Is that why you don't like her?"

"I never said I didn't like her."

"Sometimes it sounds like you don't."

Theo searched for another flat rock, then skipped it out over the water. She was sure a good shot for a girl, Kip thought, watching the rock skip three times.

"Dad says Vicky's insecure. That's why she acts so spoiled."

It was odd, Kip thought, to hear someone his own age talk about her mother as though she were a child. But then, he sometimes thought of Gram as a child.

"Sometimes, though, I wonder if Vicky really loves us." Theo looked thoughtful. "I used to think she only married Dad to get her start. He was writing for another show when they met. Vicky only had a small part. When they decided to get married he created *Destiny Jones*. That was Vicky's big break. But all this last year, I've had the feeling that she's just acting a role with Dad. Hey, what's that?'' Several yards ahead Theo had spotted three tremendous rectangular holes dug into the dunes. Each one was about six times the length of the Stanhope house. A bright red sign behind them said MARENACK.

"They're digging foundations for a new resort."

Theo suddenly remembered the signs she'd seen driving in from the airport. "Funny," she said. "In New York, you'd have to tear a building down to find the space to build another."

"Let's look in it. Maybe we'll find some arrowheads." Kip squatted and slid down into the excavation.

"Pretty awful, if you ask me, to stick a big building right out here on the beach," Theo said. "It'll ruin everything." She looked around at the powdery dunes and the deep blue sea running off to the horizon. She had an eerie sense of timelessness, as if she'd been looking across this sea for centuries.

"Coming?" Kip called back up to her.

Theo sighed and slid down into the hole. "Why would you find arrowheads here?" She followed Kip as he paced the length of the excavation.

"This part of the island's called the Madequecham. Indians used to live here."

"I once found an Indian-head nickel in Central Park. You know, the ones with the buffalo on the back."

Kip grinned. "That's not so old. They used Indian-head nickels when my dad was growing up."

"I know," Theo said thoughtfully. "But I was just

thinking, Indians used to live on Manhattan, too, hundreds of years ago. Wouldn't it be awful if the same thing happened here?''

"What do you mean?" Kip stooped to turn over a pile of dirt.

"You know, if all this beautiful land got covered over with buildings." Theo thought of the meadow of grazing sheep she'd seen from Norma's cab, with its pond and its willows and wildflowers, all to be bulldozed under for a Marenack resort.

"As a matter of fact, some folks on the island are worried that just might happen."

"But why?" Theo asked. "Aren't there enough hotels on the island already?"

"Each summer more and more people visit. It's getting to be a very popular place." Kip said this more with annoyance than pride. "The front of the island's already swarming with tourists. Have you been into town yet?"

"No. But I've heard it's pretty, with cobblestone streets and all the old houses."

"When you can *see* the streets," Kip said wryly. "That's where most of the tourists hang out. By the end of the month, Main Street will be so crammed my parents won't even go there. And forget the beaches on the other side of the island. The whole place gets like a carnival. And now, with this Marenack building up the back shore, there'll be mobs out here pretty soon. The view's not going to be too great either, with hotels all up and down the beach."

Theo frowned at the thought of this view being

blotted out by a building. Having lived her whole life in Manhattan, she was surprised that this even bothered her. But it did. There was something comfortingly familiar about this untouched stretch of beachfront, something that made her feel more at home than she'd ever felt on the street where she grew up. She realized that she'd never been anywhere before that was so nearly what it had been before people came.

"I love it here," she finally said. "It'll be hard when I have to leave. New York, the street where I live, and my school, they hardly seem real since I've been here."

"Hey, that reminds me. How come *you're* not in school?" Kip asked.

"We got out a week ago Wednesday. It's a private school." Theo looked back at the deep foundation and frowned. It was like a wound, she thought, an ugly dark scar against the white sand. She turned and followed Kip up the bulldozer tracks and out the other side. Again, as her eyes met the glassy sea and the white clouds banked up against the horizon, she had the strange but pleasant feeling that she'd looked out on this view many, many times before.

8 Something in the Air

Back on the Stanhopes' deck, Theo's father still hunched at his typewriter, pecking away. Balls of crumpled paper spilled over the table and across the floor.

"Still stuck?" Theo asked, starting up the stairs. Her father nodded and wearily rubbed his eyes.

"I don't know whether to have Alex die in a car crash or let Rita shoot him for cheating on her. The shooting could lead to some good courtroom drama for Destiny. But if he dies accidentally, it just means one episode about the inheritance, and I hoped to get a little more mileage out of this. He's legally still married to Rita, so without the murder I can't take it much further." Mr. Benedict scratched his head.

"See what I mean?" Theo whispered to Kip. "Believe me, you wouldn't want to watch it."

The doorbell sounded from inside the house.

"It's about time." Vicky's voice drifted out from the living room. "Glue on a smile and let the man . . . oh, Will!" She stood at the door to the deck, frowning. "Honestly, what's the matter with you? I told you to dress twenty minutes ago."

Mr. Benedict began to stand.

"Never mind," she said with annoyance, "I'll let him in myself." A few moments later, she breezed out to the deck with a man in tow. He was tall and thin, with jet-black hair and a deep tan that contrasted sharply with icy gray eyes. Kip recognized him immediately as Aron's father.

"Will," Vicky started in her husky voice, depositing several boxes on top of the typewriter and draping one silky arm around Mr. Benedict's neck, "this is Mr. Amonti. His wife chairs their chapter of the club."

Kip wondered what Aron's father was doing here. In his soiled carpenter's pants and denim shirt stained with sweat, the man looked about as out of place as Kip felt.

"Mr. Amonti arranged for the house," Vicky added, discreetly nudging her husband.

"Remarkable place." Mr. Benedict extended his hand to shake Mr. Amonti's. "Almost feels like a yacht."

"It was built to give that impression." Mr. Amonti returned the handshake firmly.

"These gifts are from the club members, Will. There's even one for Theda." Vicky turned back to Mr. Amonti. "How thoughtful of you to think of her."

"Please, go ahead and open them," Mr. Amonti said and gestured toward the packages. Kip suddenly felt as if he were watching a play.

"Come here, Theda, this one's for you." Vicky beckoned to Theo.

Theo crossed the deck and accepted the box from Vicky. An expression of wonderment crossed her face when she pulled off the lid. "It's beautiful," she said. The surprise in her voice was genuine. From the box she produced a thin necklace of shells with a pendant at the bottom. The shells were every color of the rainbow, but the pendant's stone was a velvety black. Mr. Amonti smiled with pleasure when she slipped it on. While her parents opened their gifts, Theo crossed the deck to show Kip.

Vicky's box contained a pink silk scarf spotted with tiny green crabs. Theo's father was given a tiepin shaped like a whale.

"I don't think I can take this sun." Vicky was fanning herself with Mr. Benedict's script. "Why don't we discuss the appearance inside? Will, come in and make us a drink.'' She began to lead Mr. Amonti in by the arm.

"Theo and Kip? Want to join us?'' Mr. Benedict paused by the door.

"Come on.'' Theo tugged Kip by the elbow. "Dad makes this great drink with grenadine. You'll love it.''

Kip followed her in, taking a seat next to her on the velvet couch. Mr. Benedict was at the bar mixing drinks. Mr. Amonti stood with Vicky by the piano.

"The Amontis would like us to join them for dinner, Will. At the . . .'' Vicky looked lost for a moment.

"The Gone-Fish-Inn,'' Mr. Amonti filled in. Kip saw the man glance at Theo with an odd, unreadable expression. Theo was fidgeting with the pendant. "I hope you'll bring Theda, too,'' he added.

"Theo?'' Mr. Benedict caught her eye. "Want to come along?''

"Sure.'' Theo nodded, then turned back to studying the pendant.

"Can any of you play?'' Mr. Amonti set his glass on top of the piano.

"Theo does.'' Mr. Benedict finished passing the drinks, then took a seat by Kip on the couch. Kip covered the patch on his knee with one hand, feeling even more out of place than before. "Been at it for quite a while now — since you were six, is that right, Theo?''

"I'd like to hear you play,'' Mr. Amonti said amiably.

"When will the appearance be?'' Vicky asked,

abruptly changing the subject. Mr. Amonti turned to her, but Kip noticed that his gaze kept returning to Theo while he discussed the fan club with Vicky.

"Who is *that?*" Kip heard Vicky's voice rise above the others, and, turning, he thought for a moment she was looking right at him. He felt his face go red as Theo and her father turned toward him too.

"No, that." Vicky jabbed a finger toward the window behind Kip. "That old woman." She turned to Mr. Amonti, who suddenly looked very uncomfortable. Theo, Mr. Benedict, and Kip all swiveled their heads around to look out the window. Kip's grandmother was standing outside by a rosebush, staring in. She was still in her nightgown. Her hand went to one of the branches and broke it off. Why did Gram have to wander down here, of all places? Kip thought with embarrassment.

"Will, dear, perhaps you should call the police. These are private grounds, and she does look a bit, ah, peculiar," Vicky observed icily. Kip turned and glared at her.

"She's *not* peculiar. She's my grandmother."

Vicky's mouth puckered into a tiny round hole. "Oh," she said softly, clapping her hands together. "Well, then, no harm done. But do ask her not to pick the roses."

"Don't worry," Kip mumbled, heading out the door.

"Who is that person?" Vicky looked disapprovingly after him.

"A friend of mine," Theo muttered, watching Kip lead Gram back up the beach. Vicky does it every time she opens her mouth, Theo brooded — she spoils everything. Then she felt the anger bristling again at the back of her mind.

"The woman had a stroke several years ago," Theo heard Mr. Amonti say behind her. "Behaves oddly at times. Sad, really."

"So unpleasant, growing old," Vicky said thoughtfully. Theo felt her face go hot, then there it was, the same odd vibration she'd felt in the airplane, tingling down her spine. As she shifted in her seat, a faint buzzing noise, like the sound of an angry fly, stirred the air. Mr. Amonti's brow creased and he knotted his fingers together. Then, without warning, the crystal glass Vicky held shattered in her hand. Vicky jerked back her arm as if she'd been stung. Theo's father rushed across the room.

"Did it cut you?" He reached for her hand. Vicky shook it away.

"I'm all right," she said with annoyance. "Don't make a fuss."

"What happened?" Mr. Benedict stooped to pick up the glass.

"Might have been a jet breaking the sound barrier," Mr. Amonti suggested. "I've seen it happen before."

"But we would have heard it. That sort of thing makes a lot of noise. Maybe the glass was cracked and you held it too tightly. This is delicate crystal." Theo's father dumped the shards in a wastebasket and brushed off his hands. There *had* been some sort of sound, Theo thought as she watched Vicky pour herself another drink, her hands shaking.

"What are you staring at?" she said to Theo sharply.

"Why don't you make yourself useful and play the piano for Mr. Amonti? God knows, you practice enough." She set her drink on the piano and beckoned to Theo.

Theo crossed the room and sat stiffly at the bench. For a moment she stared at the polished keys. Then she raised both hands and began to play, a smile creeping across her face.

"Theda, please, not that piece. Can't you play something more soothing?" Vicky attempted a smile at Mr. Amonti. "She's a very energetic child," she explained, but Mr. Amonti did not seem to hear. He was staring out the window after Kip and Gram, his eyes dark with worry.

Gram was still holding the branch from the Stanhopes' rosebush while Kip led her gently by the arm. The ocean breeze blew the blossoms off the stems, scattering the petals behind them in the sand. Several times she glanced back over her shoulder at the window where Mr. Amonti stood.

"Man two," Gram mumbled, seeming to have no real interest in the roses. By the time they reached home, the stems were nearly bare.

Kip left Gram in her rocker on the porch and started through the house.

"Kip? Is that you?" His mother's voice sailed out from the kitchen. She was kneeling on the counter, washing the window above the sink. "Where were you?" she asked as Kip's head disappeared inside the refrigerator.

"I met those people renting the Stanhopes'." He re-emerged with a carton of milk in one hand and a pickle jar in the other.

"Oh? What are they like?"

"Norma was right," Kip replied gloomily. "The mother is Boat Basin, all the way."

Mrs. Sheridan emptied a pail of gray water into the sink. "Do me a favor, Kip, and bring Gram in. I want to wash her hair before starting lunch."

Outside on the porch Gram rocked back and forth, her eyes closed, the rose stems scattered in her lap. No point telling Mom about it, Kip thought, picking them up and tossing them over the railing.

"Mom wants to wash your hair," he said gently, prodding her from the chair. Gram blinked open her eyes and struggled to her feet as though she had been asleep.

In the kitchen, Kip's mother had the spray hose hooked to the faucet, her hand under the running water as she adjusted the temperature. Gram shuffled across to the sink.

"Like the warm water, eh, Gram?" Mrs. Sheridan smiled at her brightly.

Kip poured himself a glass of milk and began to eat a pickle. After a moment he remembered the paper he'd taken from Gram's pocket. He pulled it out and flattened it on the table. "Mom, have you ever seen this before?" he asked.

"I can't look now, Kip. What is it?"

"Something Gram had yesterday. I think it's a list of Indian symbols."

"Probably something she tucked away, from the

Historical Society. Now and then I find things like that hidden in her room. You know Gram.'' Mrs. Sheridan vigorously worked the lather through Gram's hair. Gram smiled like a cat napping in the sun.

"Come on, Pocahontas, bend forward.'' Kip's mother tilted Gram's head over the sink and rinsed out her hair.

"I wonder what they mean.'' Kip studied the symbols. And the numbers in the corner, what could they stand for? he wondered.

"I usually send those things back to the Historical Society when I find them.'' Mrs. Sheridan turned off the water and briskly dried Gram's hair. "You know, Norma's sister runs their library now. She used to work under Gram.'' Kip's mother led Gram to a chair by the table and wrapped her head in a towel.

Gram suddenly narrowed her eyes and frowned. "Man two,'' she exclaimed. She was frowning at the paper with the symbols. Kip and his mother exchanged glances.

"What is she trying to say?'' Kip asked.

Mrs. Sheridan rubbed Gram's shoulder. "God knows. Poor Gram. It must be awful not to be understood. Want to work on your puzzle, Gram?''

Gram stared at the paper till Kip put it back in his pocket. When Mrs. Sheridan set the puzzle before her, Gram's frown vanished and her speckled hands began to pick at the pieces, trying them one way and then another until they locked into place.

"I'll start lunch in a minute. I just want to take a few things off the line.'' Mrs. Sheridan picked up the laundry basket and went out the back door. It banged behind her, jarring the flies from the screen. They buzzed angrily for a few seconds, then settled again, like tiny winged emeralds embroidered onto the screen.

Kip glanced across at Gram. "Man two?" he asked softly, watching Gram fit a blue piece into a patch of sea.

This wasn't the first time Vicky had driven off one of her friends, Theo thought dismally as she changed into her swimsuit. She wished she at least knew Kip's last name or where he lived so she could apologize.

"Going to lie out in the sun?" Mr. Benedict asked her as she crossed the deck.

"I think I'll go for a swim." Still angry and hot, Theo looked out at the water. The rolling, white-capped waves seemed almost to be beckoning.

"Remember what Norma Pocket told us about the undertow. Be sure you stick to the sandbars," Mr. Benedict called out as she bounded down the stairs.

Theo ran across the scorching sand and waded along the shore. Seaweed, twigs, and shells churned beneath the pounding surf. Once more, she began to feel as though something was watching her. A gull cried overhead. Theo followed it with her gaze as it glided over the dunes. What was it, what gave her this feeling?

Farther along, the water paled to aqua and lapped the shore gently. Picking out a spot on the beach above the sandbar, Theo threw down her towel and slipped on her face mask. She waded out till it was deep enough to swim, then held her breath and dove beneath the water.

Her shadow coasted over the rippled sand below her

as schools of tiny fish darted out of her path. Surfacing now and again for air, she explored the sandbar, following a hermit crab dragging its shell, till it left it for one that was larger; picking up starfish and sand dollars; and watching the fish flashing silver in the sun veer timidly around her. When she grew tired, she slipped over onto her back and floated, her eyes closed and the sun warm on her face.

She did not know how long she'd been floating when she felt something grope at her ankle. She jerked her foot back, twisting around to look beneath her. But the water here was dark and murky, and she saw, in a moment of panic, that she'd drifted out beyond the sandbar and was caught in a current angling away from the beach. Kicking furiously, pulling herself forward with quick cutting strokes, she swam with her eyes locked on the pale stretch of sandbar ahead.

After several minutes her toes touched bottom. She stood still, catching her breath, then looked back uneasily as she hurried toward shore. What was it, Theo wondered, what had touched her? Shuddering, she remembered how it felt, almost like the grip of a hand. One good thing, she thought to herself. If it *hadn't* touched her, she might have been swept out to sea.

Wading out of the water, Theo followed with her eyes the slope of the sandbar down into the murky shadows. Rippling in the undercurrent were tentacles of kelp, their ropy stalks disappearing into the darkness. Her breath caught as she spotted something large and gray moving in the seaweed — something with the same twiglike arms she'd seen thrashing in the surf the day before.

Then the kelp swirled in the current and the creature vanished.

Shivering now, Theo wrapped her towel around her and sat in the sand. What *was* that thing? she wondered, hunching her shoulders and pulling the towel tighter. The pendant Mr. Amonti had given her felt like ice against her chest. Theo pulled it out from under the towel and looked at it closely. Odd, she thought. When she'd looked at the stone in the house it had seemed to be polished smooth. But now she could make out a network of lines etched in a sort of design. She wondered why she hadn't noticed this before.

The pendant swayed from her neck as her eyes returned to the sandbar and searched the darker water along the edge. That wave yesterday might have been an illusion, but not this, she told herself. Something out there had touched her, and now she had the nagging feeling that it was watching. In spite of the hot sun beating down, Theo continued to shiver.

9 A Room Full of Fire

"I hope their taste in food is better than their taste in gifts. That scarf with the crab print was positively ridiculous." Vicky was staring at herself in a compact in front of the entrance to the Gone-Fish-Inn. She smoothed out a blotch of make-up on the tip of her nose, then pushed on her dark glasses.

"I liked mine." Theo looked thoughtfully again at the pattern etched in her pendant.

"All right, I'm ready. Let's get this over with." Vicky loosened her shawl so it dipped below one shoulder. Mr. Benedict held the door and then followed them in.

The three of them paused in the entry and surveyed the long room.

"Not bad. It's actually charming," Vicky remarked as she studied the decor. The restaurant was built out over the harbor. Lighted yachts bobbed outside the windows. "Shall we stop in the cocktail lounge? I could use a drink before we go in to meet them."

"Vicky, we're already forty minutes late." Mr. Benedict glanced at his watch.

"I'm hungry," Theo mumbled, knowing that once Vicky set foot in the lounge, dinner would be forgotten.

"Is that all you can think of?" Vicky began fussing with Theo's hair.

"It's a restaurant, Vicky. What is she supposed to think of?" Mr. Benedict glanced around for a sign of the Amontis.

"The ambience. The music. The candlelight. Theda, stop squirming."

"Those candles look like bug lights to me. Kip says the greenheads are wicked this time of year." Theo squinted through the dimly lit dining room at the squat red candles on the tables. Vicky raised one eyebrow at her.

"Really, Theda, I wish you'd give some attention to your appearance."

"You're hurting me." Theo tried to twist away.

"I told you to stop squirming. Now you've got your hair caught in my bracelet."

"There he is." Mr. Benedict waved across the room to Mr. Amonti.

"Now just don't you embarrass me," Vicky mumbled. Theo winced as Vicky tugged her bracelet free.

"Glad you could make it. We almost gave up." Mr. Amonti shook Mr. Benedict's hand. "I hope you brought an appetite." He turned his attention to Theo.

"I'm starving," she replied, smiling shyly while rubbing the sore spot on her head.

Mr. Amonti smiled back warmly and offered her his arm. "Our table is over by the windows. I thought you might like to watch the boats."

"That's *just* what I wanted to do." Theo beamed up at the man as she took his arm and accompanied him across the crowded room, her parents following behind. "I love the pendant, Mr. Amonti, and I wanted to ask" — Theo held up the stone to show him the design — "do you know if this stands for anything special, like an insignia or something?"

"I believe it's just ornamental," he replied, letting go of her arm as they approached a small table by the windows. "This is Theda Benedict," he addressed a thin dark woman with braided hair who stood to greet them.

"I've been looking forward to meeting you, Theda. I'm Mrs. Amonti." The woman took Theo's hand and clasped it warmly.

Looking forward to meeting *me?* Well, *that's* a first,

with Vicky around, Theo thought to herself.

"Theda, would you sit by me?" Mrs. Amonti pulled out a chair and smiled at her brightly. "I'm anxious to hear what you think of our little island."

"You can call me Theo. Everyone does." Theo sat down beside her. Already she felt as drawn to these people as she had to Norma Pocket. While Mrs. Amonti greeted Theo's parents, Theo studied the menu.

"Why don't we sit over there by the stage?" she heard Vicky ask. Theo's stomach rumbled noisily. Vicky shot her a glance.

"I thought you'd like the privacy." Mr. Amonti sounded disappointed.

"Nonsense." Vicky gathered up her shawl. "I'm used to crowds. And we can't see a thing from way over here."

She means no one can see *her* from here, Theo thought, putting down the menu.

"But the view of the harbor . . ." Mrs. Amonti began, but Vicky had turned her back and was leading Theo's father toward a table by the stage. A bald little man crooned behind a piano. His odd warbly voice, pointy nose, and elbows jutting out like wings reminded Theo of a bird.

"*I* like looking at the harbor," Theo remarked, feeling badly for the Amontis. "I'd much rather sit here and watch the boats."

"Then you will," Mrs. Amonti said kindly. "We'll straighten it out with your father."

Theo leaned back and watched the Amontis moving after her parents. She saw Vicky remove her dark glasses and heard the whispers start up around the room, moving from one table to the next like wind rustling through grass. In minutes, Vicky was surrounded by tourists asking for autographs. Theo's father glanced back as Mrs. Amonti took his arm. Spotting Theo, he nodded and smiled weakly, then disappeared in the throng. Theo knew he would have liked the view of the harbor, too. Darn Vicky, Theo brooded, she never thinks about what other people want.

A waiter approached Theo's table and flipped out his pad. "Mr. Amonti said to order anything you like," he told Theo.

Theo closed the menu. "I don't know. I guess just a tuna sandwich and a glass of milk." Just thinking about Vicky took away her appetite. Glancing back across the room, she saw that the birdlike man had stopped playing and was sitting at the bar. Her parents and the Amontis were hidden behind a crowd of Vicky's admirers. More customers began to drift through the doors. If nothing else, Vicky was good for business, Theo thought to herself. She turned her gaze back to the window.

When the waiter returned with her order, Theo heard the chair across from her scrape the floor. Looking up, she saw a dark, lanky boy with black hair and deep, piercing eyes. His face seemed somehow familiar. Wasn't this the boy with the bike she'd seen talking to Norma? Theo wondered.

"Guess this isn't much fun for you." The boy stood tentatively above the drawn-out chair. "I'm Aron Amonti. I was supposed to meet you all here, but I guess . . ." He glanced at the crowd around Vicky's table.

"It's O.K. I'm used to it." Theo took a sip of her milk. "So, are you a fan of Vicky's, too?" she asked, still uncertain if this was the same boy.

"Not really," Aron answered, sitting down.

"But your parents are." Theo nibbled at her sandwich.

"I guess." Aron was staring at her. There was something strange about the boy's eyes. They were the same odd, smoky gray as Norma's, but beneath the shadow of his brow they seemed almost to look through her. Theo looked down at her sandwich. She didn't mind the company, but she wished he wouldn't stare.

"I read *Moby-Dick* in school this year," she said brightly. "It's exciting to think it all happened right here."

"I never read it." Aron finally lowered his eyes.

"But it's all about whaling, and takes place —"

"I know," Aron interrupted, knotting his fingers together. "I just don't like stories about whaling."

"But why? *Moby-Dick* made it sound so exciting."

"Because," Aron said softly, "whales are gentle, and they're very smart, and it seems an awful waste of life just to light a lamp or make lipstick and shoe polish. But it won't go on much longer."

"That's good," Theo remarked. "I didn't know they were used for things like that. It *is* awful."

"It won't go on much longer," Aron continued, "because whales will soon be extinct. There are hardly any left in this part of the sea, and almost none around the island." There was a dullness to his voice. "So much of the old world is dying."

"The old world?" Theo asked, feeling oddly drawn toward Aron and his strange, hypnotic voice.

"The way things were, the way the world was meant to be. Long before the men who whaled came here." He looked up at her. "Have you explored much of the island?" he asked.

"Only the Madequecham. What's that resort they're building out there?"

"Another Marenack," Aron said in a flat, disapproving voice.

"The beach out there is so beautiful. They should leave it alone." As Theo said this, she thought she caught the barest hint of a smile on his face.

"Developers and tourists don't much care about the island. They don't think twice about messing things up."

"That's not true," Theo said defensively. "I'm a tourist, and I don't feel that way."

"I know that," Aron said more gently. "But still, many do. Many more than you'd think. And the developers," Aron said with a sigh, "they're the real problem, the way they're building over the land, drawing in more and more tourists. They're crowding us out and ruining the land. If it goes on like this, the island will just be one huge resort. The dunes, the meadowlands, they'll all disappear."

"But that's just what makes it so wonderful here." Theo found herself suddenly angry.

"*We* know that. But not everyone feels the same way." The way Aron said *we* made Theo feel strange

The boy's eyes held her fixed in his gaze. "Till now, nothing's ever been built on the Madequecham," he continued. "But by next summer that whole stretch of beachfront will be built over."

"Marenack?" Theo asked.

Aron nodded, glancing through the window at the gently rocking boats. "That one developer now owns more of Nantucket than all the islanders combined."

"How did Marenack get all the land?" Theo asked.

"When he first came in and made his bids, some islanders saw it as their big chance to get rich. Not everyone who lives here loves the island like we do."

That *we,* and the way Aron looked at her, gave Theo the odd feeling he was including her.

"Some people love money much more," he went on. "It's a kind of sickness. And once a few people started selling, it caught like wildfire. Not many people want to live in the shadow of a Marenack development. Most of the islanders who own land are selling out."

"I wonder what it was like before there was anyone on the island?" Theo said wistfully.

"Many parts, like the back shore and the moors, are just the way they were. Have you seen the hill land?"

"No. Where's that?"

"At the center of the island. The Indians used to live there. All that land is pretty much the same. The Indians never pretended to own it. That's how the colonists took over so easily. Like the developers today." Aron gazed out at the harbor. "Some of that land is sacred, places where they buried their dead. There's a rumor that Marenack plans to build on that ground, too."

"Can't anyone stop him?" Theo asked.

"One group tried to outbid him for the land. They wanted to turn the wild parts of the island into a nature preserve."

"What happened?"

"They didn't have enough money."

"So that's *it?*" Theo's anger surprised her. For a moment Aron just stared at her with a look she could almost feel, as if they were joined together in some strange way. She wanted to turn away, but his gray eyes held her, watching, reaching, pulling her in and reflecting back her anger. Suddenly a light flickered at the back of her mind, and she felt the heat of her anger rising. Then the light seemed to pour out of her, spreading into the room, beyond Aron, out over the tables, where it glowed in the faces around her. It lit up the hollow red caves of mouths, and the chatter, the chewing, and the sounds of laughter swelled through the air, growing louder. Then she felt the light burn like a fire racing down her spine, and the room suddenly exploded with cries and flames.

Theo squeezed her eyes shut and covered her ears. There was a sudden rushing sound in her head, and the air grew cool. Shaking, sucking in her breath, she opened her eyes again, slowly. Now people seemed to float above their seats in a murky, fluid darkness, their faces pale and bloated and their clothing charred. Theo leaned toward the table and gripped it tightly, trying to scream, but she felt her mouth fill with water, with a salty taste like the sea, and everything began to spin as if caught in a whirlpool.

Black wings, seaweed snakes, and stumps with crooked arms rushed by. Then an icy, numbing undertow dragged her down and drowned her in darkness.

10 The Mind Thieves

"Theo . . . Theo!" A hand shook her roughly. Theo cracked open her eyes, and for a moment she thought her father was kneeling on the wall; but the wall was carpeted, and as her head cleared she saw that she was sprawled on her side on the floor, her father crouching above her.

"What happened?" he asked. The waiter and the Amontis crowded behind him. She pulled herself up, struggling to find words to describe the burning heat, the smothering feeling.

"Are you O.K.?" Mr. Benedict brushed a hand against her flushed cheek.

"I . . . I felt like I couldn't breathe." She shook her head. "I was talking to Aron . . . it got so hot." She glanced around.

"Who?" her father asked.

"Aron Amonti. He was just . . ."

"Aron went home, dear. He left a few minutes before you fainted." Mrs. Amonti was looking down at her. Her eyes were gray, like Aron's, but softer.

"It *is* rather hot in here." Her father helped her up "Come on, let's get you outside for some air."

The Amontis waited with her on the sidewalk while her father went back in for Vicky. "It gets very stuffy in there when it's crowded," Mrs. Amonti said as she stroked Theo's hair.

What happened in there? Theo wondered. Aron was talking, then . . .

"You shouldn't be standing, dear. Come sit on the curb." Mrs. Amonti helped her to the street while her husband went to fetch a cab. Theo shivered as she sat, straining to remember. Something with light and . . . but now her mind felt blocked, as if a wall were shutting out the event. She stared at the street, at the litter in the gutter, at the feet of people passing. The night air was full of loud music and laughter. She would feel better when she got back to their house at Tom Nevers Head, to the quiet, open stretch of sand and sea.

"Here they are," Mrs. Amonti said.

Theo looked back toward the restaurant. Vicky emerged, accompanied by several fans holding out menus and checks for autographs. Mr. Benedict walked down to the curb just as Mr. Amonti returned with a cab. The Amontis bid them goodnight, and Theo's father helped her into the back of the cab. Norma Pocket sat behind the wheel studying Theo in the rearview mirror.

"You're sure you're O.K.?" Mr. Benedict pressed Theo's hand. Theo nodded, but she still felt shaken.

"How did it happen?" He brushed the hair back from her forehead.

"I don't know." Theo shrugged, still straining to recall. Was it water behind the wall? But the heat, like a fire . . . "I was hot," she said.

Norma Pocket turned in her seat. Theo felt the woman's eyes on her.

"That's all, I just felt really hot." Why can't I remember? she wondered with frustration.

"It *was* awfully warm." Mr. Benedict rolled down his window. "Did you get anything to eat?"

"A little," Theo answered. "Half a sandwich."

"That's all?"

"I wasn't very hungry."

"Did you eat any lunch?"

"Not really. There was only smoked oysters and stuff like that, nothing I wanted to eat."

"We'll go shopping in the morning. What's keeping her?" he said impatiently, glancing out at Vicky having her picture taken with the owner beneath the sign of the restaurant.

"So, what happened?" Vicky frowned at Theo as she finally climbed into the cab.

"She's hardly eaten anything today," Mr. Benedict answered. "Plus the heat, and the noise."

"If she doesn't eat right, she has no one to blame but herself."

"Maybe if you'd keep something besides cocktail hors d'oeuvres in the house . . ."

"We eat *out* all the time. And if you're concerned about what's in the house, then *you* do something about it. She's your . . ."

Their arguing sounded miles away. Theo struggled to remember what had happened just before she blacked out. Outside she watched the crowds of tourists drifting past her window, their faces pale in the headlights . . .

faces pale . . . floating? A stone began to loosen from the wall that blocked her memory. The cab slid toward a red light. Theo's eyes caught something glistening on the windshield, trickling down. Threads of water seemed to seep through the windows and stream from the knobs on the dashboard. The red light spreading over the street grew dim. A figure floated past the front of the cab, like someone swimming.

Theo stiffened in her seat. Norma's eyes fixed on the mirror, probing the panic in Theo's face, beginning to draw the vision away.

The car lurched as Norma braked, jolting Theo back to the present. "Watch where you're going!" a man shouted, glaring through the windshield and banging his fist on the hood. For a fleeting second, the street had looked like a world submerged in water, like the vision she'd seen beyond the deck doors her first day on the island.

The man on the street was still shouting, but Norma's eyes were fixed on Theo's reflection in the mirror. Theo turned to her father. Underwater, that was it. She opened her mouth to speak, but suddenly her thought was gone. The memory of the vision was lost, drawn away again, and she was left with the uneasy feeling that something urgent was just beyond her reach. The light turned green. Norma shifted gears, her eyes still on Theo. Theo sighed and nestled against her father's shoulder. What was it, she wondered with annoyance, what was it she had been about to say?

The crowds grew thinner as they drove toward the outskirts of town. Soon the first Marenack sign appeared.

As Theo looked at it, the things Aron had said began to come back. Why had they made her so angry? she wondered. It was bad, what was happening here, but why should it anger *her* so?

As Norma turned onto the road that led to Tom Nevers Head and the Stanhope house Theo leaned toward the window and breathed the ocean air. She stared at the lighted windows of the houses scattered along the shore. They reminded her of campfires nestled cozily between the dunes, with the rhythmic pounding of the surf beyond like a drumbeat, or the pulse of a heart. Watching the lights, she wondered which of these houses was Kip's.

Kip lay in his bed staring out the window. The crescent of a quarter moon hung like a hook in the sky. The froth on the waves below glowed white, and the night was swept with soft breezes. Beyond the dunes, the taillights of a passing car winked up at him like eyes — small red demon eyes — retreating into the night. Dust swirled up in a rosy glow as the cab hurtled down the shoreline drive. High above, invisible against the sky, black wings followed. Kip snuggled into his pillow.

"Man two," he mumbled to himself, wondering again what Gram had meant as he drifted off to sleep.

In the room below, Mr. Sheridan was speaking on the phone. Kip's mother leaned against the doorway, listening.

"It doesn't have a bug, sir, I promise you. It was all checked out yesterday." He paused. "No, it doesn't make sense. And it won't till we're up in the air." Another pause, then, in a lower voice, "Because an abnormality in the gravity would indicate a fault. Since we're sitting on a thick layer of sand and clay, that soft stuff would mold itself right over a shift. Any visible evidence of a fault would be erased." Mr. Sheridan glanced at his wife, catching the worried look in her eyes. "Sure it's possible. A shift could have been easing itself into place imperceptibly for centuries. But if it's a new one forming, these are only the foreshocks. That's why I want to go up tomorrow." A longer silence. Mr. Sheridan smiled at his wife. "Maybe no more than a few shattered windows. It would depend on where it is and the strength of the tremors. There are a thousand small quakes worldwide every day that no one feels." He paused, then in a lower voice said, "Land erosion, tidal waves, but that would be the extreme." Another long silence. "You can't predict that sort of thing. For now, all we can do is watch it . . . No, I won't talk to anyone . . . Right, I'll see you in the morning."

"Who was that?" Mrs. Sheridan asked as he dropped the phone back in its cradle.

"Chief warrant officer at the Coast Guard station out on Brant Point. He's arranging the use of the plane so I can measure the ground pull."

"I thought you missed Evelyn's party to do that this afternoon."

"Commander Hardy was off the island. He didn't see the report I filed till just now. We couldn't get one of their planes without his approval . . . Sorry about the party, Jinny."

"George, if you knew you weren't getting the plane, why didn't you meet me?"

"The seismograph acted up again. I wanted to keep an eye on it. I didn't want to worry you."

"George, just how serious is it?" Mrs. Sheridan sounded nervous.

"Won't know till we take the plane up. Look, Jinny, I don't want you to worry about it. For all we know, this thing could be so minor we may never hear from it again. By the way, Hardy doesn't want us talking about it with anyone. Not even Kip. He doesn't want quake rumors starting up."

"But George, on the phone you said —"

"Jinny," he interrupted, "there are scores of faults riddling the globe. Only a handful ever cause any damage. This thing's probably totally benign."

Theo fell asleep to the muffled strains of her parents quarreling in the other room. Again the boy with the upstretched arms appeared in her dreams. But now a second figure stood beside him, tall and slender in a flowing skirt. The woman also raised her hands, clasping one of the boy's. Theo drifted toward the grassy plot where they stood. But then the earth began to break open as before, and the stones rose again like gravestones, then higher, till the ground and the figures vanished beneath them.

A clicking sound crept into Theo's mind. The stones changed into tall buildings, and behind them a clockface rose up like the sun. At the center of the clockface she saw her own reflection, but it, too, was changing.

The eyes turned wild and fiery, and horns twisted up from the brow. A serpent's tongue flicked over the lips, and when Theo opened her mouth to scream, the jaw snapped open with an explosion of fire. The hand she threw out to shield herself was reflected in the clockface as a two-pronged claw.

Theo awoke in a cold sweat, her arms and legs entangled in the sheets. It was a dream, she told herself as she kicked free from the covers and breathed deeply. Why was she having these terrible dreams? A warm, humid breeze poured through the open window. Theo stared out at the moon, listening to a faint, rhythmic clicking in the air. The sound seemed to come from the clock in the hall. Its steady beat began to lull her back to sleep. As the strange dream receded the clicking grew weaker, as if one drew away the other, and faded off into the night.

A track through the sand led away from beneath Theo's window down to the shore, ending where the surf bubbled over something resembling a tree stump with gnarled, branching arms. The armor of the huge gray crab shone like silver in the moonlight. Its mandibles grinding and clicking, it crawled, spiderlike, deeper into the water. The shifting tide dissolved its shell and remolded its crooked legs into human limbs.

11 Night Music

Sunday morning the beach shimmered with heat mirages. Theo squinted in the glare as she strolled along the edge of the shore, pausing now and then to stare out at the water, trying to place an odd image that kept surfacing in her mind. An image of a car with horns on the hood, driving through a street underwater. Was it from a dream? she wondered. What could it possibly mean? It's all such a muddle, she thought to herself as she looked down at the froth bubbling over her feet. She stooped to pick up a conch and held it to her ear, listening to the dull echo of the ocean. She put the large spiral shell in the beach bag slung over her shoulder. The bag was already bulging with sea glass, bits of driftwood, and smaller shells.

It was funny, Theo thought, as beautiful as the island was, something here made her uneasy, made her feel somehow unsafe. The feeling that she was being watched, the fainting in the restaurant, her inability to remember things, whatever it was that had touched her beneath the water, and the vision of the wave that first day — all these things came back to mind and seemed almost like warnings. An illusion, a touch, a moment of illness: why did they disturb her so?

Her thoughts were broken by the cry of a gull high above the breakers. She squinted up at it, then closed her eyes, holding her face in the sun and the warm salty breeze, inhaling deeply. The cool water swirled around her ankles, and she sank a bit in the loose sand, imagining for a moment that she was rooted, like a tree, and drew strength from the earth through her toes. Then her uneasiness vanished, and she felt, suddenly, more completely at peace than she'd ever felt before.

Walking farther down the beach, Theo caught sight of a gray shingled roof poking up from the dunes. Kip had gone this way, so perhaps this was his house. If it was, she could apologize to him for Vicky, she decided. Moving toward it, she spotted Kip's grandmother rocking on the porch. Theo sprinted across the hot sand, then stopped at the foot of the steps as Gram halted in her rocker, leaned forward, and narrowed her eyes.

"Man two," Gram muttered, glaring at her. Theo looked up at the woman, puzzled. She had no idea what she was saying, but the tone of her voice did not sound particularly friendly. She couldn't really blame her, Theo decided, after Vicky's awful scene the day before. Gram continued to glare, till Theo self-consciously backed away from the stairs and went to look for another entrance. Circling the house, she found a door at the back.

"I'm Theo Benedict," she introduced herself through the screen to the woman inside. "I'm staying down the beach at the Stanhope place."

Mrs. Sheridan was holding a wicker basket piled to her chin with wet laundry. "I'm Kip's mother. Could you open the door for me, Theo?" After Mrs. Sheridan stepped out, Theo followed her across the yard.

"Kip biked over to the jetties to fish. He may not be back till supper." Mrs. Sheridan set the basket in the sand and began to drape sheets on the line.

"Did he say anything about yesterday?" Theo asked.

"Only that he met you."

"He didn't say anything about my stepmother?"

"Not that I recall," Mrs. Sheridan replied tactfully, remembering both Kip's and Norma Pocket's comments about the woman. "Why?"

"She acts a little funny sometimes." Theo blushed. "I wanted to apologize."

"Why, what happened?" Kip's mother peered over the line at her.

"Nothing much. She gets confused, says things . . . Well, it was nice to meet you. Tell Kip to come by again, if he wants."

"I'll tell him." Mrs. Sheridan smiled. Theo turned and started back over the dunes. Kip's mother squinted at the words printed on the back of Theo's T-shirt: LIFE IS JUST A BOWL OF CHERRIES, A LITTLE SWEETNESS AND THEN IT'S THE PITS. City folk, Kip's mother thought with amusement.

Kip and his father returned home about the same time. Mr. Sheridan lingered in the kitchen while Kip went to wash up for supper.

"So you still haven't measured the ground pull?" Mrs. Sheridan was setting the table.

"No. Hardy gave me some song and dance about how busy they are. Seems the Coast Guard only has one plane available. Says he can't requisition the plane for other use until there's a break in the schedule. You'd think he'd make time, for something like this.''

"Has there been any more activity on the graph?''

"Not since yesterday.'' Mr. Sheridan sounded relieved. "Saturday's reading was a little bit higher than Friday's, had two tremors in fact, one in the afternoon and another last night. But since there was nothing today, there's a good chance that those three tremors were enough to ease the tension between the plates. Could be it's gone back to dormancy, if it's an old fau——'' Mr. Sheridan cut himself off as Kip came back into the kitchen.

"Oh, Kip, I nearly forgot.'' Mrs. Sheridan turned toward the door. "That girl who's staying at the Stanhopes' dropped by this afternoon.''

"What did she want?''

"Something about apologizing for her mother. What happened over there yesterday?''

"Nothing. Her mother was acting a little weird, that's all.'' Kip was relieved that Theo hadn't told about Gram picking the Stanhopes' roses.

"She seemed nice, Kip.'' Mrs. Sheridan turned to her husband. "Pretty as a picture with thick dark curls, George. But I could have died when she turned around. She had one of those slogan T-shirts. It said *Life's just a bowl of cherries, a little sweetness and then it's the pits.''*

"Smart girl.'' Mr. Sheridan winked at his son. Kip was grinning in spite of himself. Life is a bowl of cherries, all right, he thought. And Theo had her fill of the pits, with a crank like Vicky for a mother.

"She said to stop by if you wanted." Kip's mother pulled the fish from the broiler. "George, would you bring Gram in? She's been out on the porch all day."

"All day? Jinny, it's been awfully hot out there. All that sun can't be good for her."

"I couldn't get her to budge, George. You'd think she was guarding the house from an Indian war party, from the look on her face."

After dinner Kip strolled along the beach, watching a sheet of fog creep slowly toward the shore. He felt the air grow cooler as the light in the sky grew dim, and, picking up his pace, he soon heard music drifting down from the Stanhope house.

Kip quietly climbed the stairs to the deck and paused before the sliding glass doors. Theo was sitting at the piano engrossed in her music. In some ways the music, with its cricketlike trills, its bass of bullfrogs, and its plinking sounds like rain, reminded Kip of the moors. He watched Theo's fingers with fascination. Every few seconds they would fly up and down the keyboard in a blur. Now and then she'd raise both hands, pause a moment, then bring them down with such force that the floor of the deck would vibrate beneath his feet.

Kip rapped lightly on the glass. Theo looked up, hands poised in midair, her face dimly lit by a candle burning on the piano.

"I thought you might be mad at me," she said as Kip slid open the door.

He shook his head. After all, it wasn't Theo's fault

that Vicky acted the way she did. "Where are your folks?" he asked.

"Vicky's meeting her fan club tonight."

As Kip walked around the piano bench, he saw that Theo was wearing the cherry T-shirt. "How come you're always wearing things with stuff written all over them?" he asked as he sat down beside her.

"It lets people know how I feel. You know, even when I'm not doing *any*thing, Vicky makes me feel like I'm doing something wrong." Theo sighed.

"She seemed O.K. with you yesterday, before that thing happened with Gram."

"That was all a show for Mr. Amonti. She's never like that when we're alone, and she's been a pain ever since we got here. Dad and I want to stay three weeks, but Vicky says she can't stand it. Vicky's bored. She hates the beach. The house is too far from town. The town's too hokey, there's nothing to do. She wants to go out, she wants to stay in. Now she wants to go home. All she does is complain all day. I'm beginning to think she's only happy when she's making everyone miserable."

"Does that mean you might be leaving soon?"

"Who knows?" Theo shrugged, turning back to the piano. "She changes her mind so often, we never know from one minute to the next." She plunked a few keys halfheartedly.

"What were you playing before?" Kip asked.

"This?" Theo did the trill that sounded like crickets. Kip nodded. "It's called 'The Night's Music.' It's by this great composer named Bartók. It's great to play when you're bugged about something, because of all the banging, but I don't really play it that well.''

"It sounded great to me." Kip watched in fascination as her hands moved over the keys.

Theo laughed. "Tell that to my piano teacher. She calls me Cliburn-Godzilla. Technique, with all the feeling of a dinosaur.''

"Wait a minute.'' He reached for the pendant dangling from Theo's neck as it swayed above the keys. "Is this the necklace Mr. Amonti gave you yesterday?''

"Isn't it neat?'' She slipped it off and handed it to him.

"This thing on the back. I didn't see it yesterday.'' He studied the symbol inscribed on one side of the pendant.

"Mr. Amonti said it's just ornamental. It's funny, yesterday I could hardly see it either. The lines just seemed like little scratches. Then last night I noticed how deep they really were.''

"It's Indian.'' Kip handed it back.

"How do you know that?''

"The symbol. I've seen it before, on a piece of paper Gram had. I figured out it was Indian because another symbol on the paper is the same as an old Indian carving on a rock in the middle of the island.''

"Do you think it means something?'' Theo held the pendant to the candle. The deep grooves filled with shadows as black as ink.

"I don't know. But there's this place in town where my grandmother used to work. It's the Nantucket Historical Society. They could probably tell us there.''

''When can we go?'' Theo looked at the pendant with renewed interest.

''You could meet me after school tomorrow. Did you bring a bicycle?''

''On the plane? There was barely enough room for people.'' Theo grinned, slipping the pendant back on. ''Can't we walk?''

''It'd take a while. But maybe you could rent one. There are places down by the ferry wharf that rent out bikes and mopeds.''

''I'll ask my dad.'' Theo turned back to the piano and began to play again.

''You know, that thing you're playing, 'The Night's Music,' reminds me a lot of the moors.'' Kip looked thoughtfully at the flickering candle. It was the only light in the room, and it seemed to grow brighter as the darkening night hugged the windows.

''The moors? Like in England?'' Theo asked, still playing.

''I don't know what the moors are in England, but we've got moors right here. That's where the rock with the symbol is.''

''Will you show them to me? After we go to that society?''

''If you teach me something on the piano,'' Kip said shyly.

''How about a duet?'' Theo offered.

''If it's not too hard. Remember, I've never even touched one of these things before.''

''This piece is a cinch.'' Theo took his hands, then

spread his fingers into position over the keys. "Just keep them like that and count along with me to five. Every time we say two and five, just push them down on the keys. I'll take care of the rest."

After they were at it for a while, Theo taught him the words that went with the song. "I made up the music myself, but I got the words from a poem by Emily Dickinson. I dedicated it to Vicky."

Kip nodded, but kept his eyes glued to the keyboard, struggling not to miss a beat. Theo began to sing:

> *I'm nobody! Who are you?*
> *Are you nobody, too?*
> *Then there's a pair of us!*
> *Don't tell! They'd banish us, you know.*
>
> *How dreary to be somebody!*
> *How public, like a frog*
> *To tell your name the livelong June*
> *To an admiring bog!*

Then they sang it together, banging away at the keys, side by side, over and over, right up till the candle on the piano burned itself out. The room went suddenly dark and Kip's hands froze. A moment later he heard a door open, then lights flashed on in the hall.

"Theda?" Vicky's voice called out. Then, spotting the two of them sitting in the dark, she stalked across the room, satin swishing and jewelry jangling. "What do you think you're doing?" Her face half in shadow, looming over them, resembled an angry moon. Kip shifted uncomfortably in his seat. Now he knew what Theo meant about feeling as though you'd done something wrong without having the slightest idea what.

"Out!" Vicky glared at Kip, pointing an iridescent fingernail toward the door. Kip slid from the bench.

"Vicky, we were only . . ."

"You think I don't know?" Vicky cut Theo off, staring menacingly at Kip.

"What's going on here?" A cab pulled away from the front of the house as Mr. Benedict stepped through the door.

"I just found your daughter alone with that boy in the dark."

Mr. Benedict looked questioningly from Theo to Kip, who lingered awkwardly by the door to the deck.

"We were only playing the piano," Theo said with frustration.

"With the lights out? Don't tell *me*, young lady!" Vicky glowered across the piano. From her breath Theo could tell she'd been drinking.

Theo tried to explain. "I was teaching Kip a song. The candle burned out just before you came in."

Mr. Benedict glanced at the wisp of smoke still trailing up from the candlestick. "It's all right, Theo. I believe you," he said.

"Brother, does she have *you* wrapped around her little finger. Well, *I* don't believe it. Not for a minute!"

"Vicky, she's only twelve."

"I was twelve once, *too*, you know. Don't think I don't remember what it was like."

"That was you, Vicky. Theo's different." Mr. Benedict sounded very tired.

"And what's *that* supposed to mean?" As Vicky turned on Theo's father, Theo gestured for Kip to leave. A little sweetness, and then it's the pits, he thought as he left the house, Vicky's accusing voice rising in anger behind him. Somewhere in the night Kip heard a deep-throated laugh. He stopped to listen. It was like the one he'd heard on the moors, only closer. Then there was a rhythmic clicking sound from down by the shore. As he turned and hurried up the moonlit beach, something slithered down from the dunes and under the Stanhopes' deck. The rustling of wings above was drowned out by the sound of the surf. Kip was well up the beach when the great black bird rushed down from the sky and lighted on the Stanhopes' roof.

Theo closed her door to shut out the sound of her parents arguing. She climbed into bed and drew the covers up over her head, but still the voices drifted in. A rush of heat hit the back of her head and went flowing down her spine — a burning, tingling sensation that made her shudder. Perspiration beaded on her forehead and her breath came in short, stifled gasps. Then she felt a deep and sudden exhaustion.

The voices of her parents receded as she drifted toward something like sleep. The heat behind her eyes now flickered like lightning, and her ears filled with a rustling sound, as if wings were beating about her face. The dreamlike image of the boy and woman with upstretched arms reappeared. Only now a man walked across the grass to join them, and together the three reached up to her. Once again the ground broke open and the gravestones rose into buildings.

Theo weaved down through shafts of gray concrete, through corridors of asphalt and vacant paved streets. She wandered through an empty world of stone, till at last she saw the boy peering back over his shoulder as he turned into an alley. At the end of the alley, Theo found a door that led to a dimly lit room. The room was cavernous, and filled with shadowlike people seated at tables. On the other side of the room she caught sight of the boy, who seemed first to stoop, then to crawl, then to slide, until he became no more than a long thin shadow of himself. Theo rushed after as he slipped through another door, but when she followed it slammed behind her, the floor gave way, and she fell into smothering darkness. It drew her down, like an undertow, into the world beyond shadows.

In a darkened room in the Institute of Oceanography, a faint scratching sound came from a small steel box. A window at the top of the box showed a needle discharging black ink in a thin straight line over a rotating sheet of paper. For less than a second, a hum sounded in the air like the buzz of a greenhead. The needle trembled, leaving a jagged break in the line, and then continued on its even path over the rotating drum.

At the Gone-Fish-Inn, a thread of light uncoiled in a darkened pantry. While the cook and his helpers bustled in the kitchen, the light hissed and flickered like a serpent's tongue. It widened and divided, slithered from an empty cupboard, and flowed down the walls in streams of fire.

12 A Sudden Storm

Paying Norma Pocket, Theo jumped from the cab and walked into the crowded bike-rental store. Tourists who had arrived on the afternoon ferry crammed impatiently against the service counter. When it was her turn, Theo picked out a bike with a basket and arranged to rent it for a week.

Standing by the door, she waved away the fumes from sputtering mopeds with a folded map of Nantucket she'd just bought. Then she opened the map and tried to orient herself, silently reading the names of each part of the island: Madequecham, Shawkemo, Quidnet, Wauwinet, Pocomo, Squam, Shimmo, Monomoy, Polpis, Quaise, Sachacha, Coskata, Miacomet, and Madaket. She knit her brows as she wondered at the musicality of these words. Alien words, yet so strangely easy and familiar somehow, as if she'd said them many times before. She still had an hour before meeting Kip at school. She stuck the map in her basket and straddled the bike, then set off for Cliff Road, a street that, according to the map, ran just above Nantucket Sound.

From the top of the ridge, she could see the bathers spread out on the beach below. Dozens of different tunes blared up from transistor radios, competing with the shouts of children and the barking of dogs. She passed by cliffside hotels, then humbler guest houses, and eventually these gave way to small private homes. Soon the distance between the houses increased, till at last she found herself on a long stretch of open country road. Theo felt a wonderful freedom away from the crowds of town. Gliding past meadows, inhaling the salty air, she could hear the steady roll of the surf, like a distant drum.

A Marenack sign loomed ahead, and just beyond it a smaller one reading BIRD SANCTUARY, PLEASE DON'T STRAY FROM THE PATH. KEEP DOGS ON LEASHES. Theo pedaled up the grade past the signs. A sliver of ocean appeared beyond the dunes at the end of the road, where another sign warned, NO TRESPASSING, TERNS NESTING. Around it, several bikes rested in the grass. Theo heard the sudden shriek of a tern and climbed to the crest of the dunes. A dog romped through the grass, snapping at the birds diving down to protect their nests. On the beach, three boys were tossing a Frisbee.

Why, Theo thought with disgust, with all the beaches to choose from, would anyone come through here? Just because a road led this way? Her eyes blurred as she watched the frantic terns dart through the air. "Shoo!" she shouted, trying to chase the dog away, but it only grew more crazed, barking after the terns and trampling their nests.

Feeling angry and helpless, Theo turned away. "There wouldn't *be* any dog if it weren't for those stupid kids," she muttered, kicking one of their bikes as she walked toward her own. "Darn people anyway, this island'd be better without them." She got on her bike and raced back down the road.

When the class finished copying the notes on Anne Frank's *Diary of a Young Girl,* Miss Feldspar erased the blackboard. Then, as was her habit at the end of her last class of the day, she wrote out the next day's date: 6-18. Then she brushed the chalk from her hands.

Kip stared at the board while the rest of the class put away their notes. June eighteenth, he thought, there's something about that date. He kept looking at the hyphenated numbers right up till the bell rang. Then it dawned on him, and he pulled Gram's piece of paper with the symbols from his pocket. It was the *way* she wrote it, with a hyphen, that jarred his memory. The numbers on Gram's paper read 6-21. Was that what the numbers meant? Kip wondered. Had Gram written down a date? June twenty-first, that was four days from now. But surely, Kip thought, Gram couldn't have meant *this* June twenty-first. The paper with the symbols was old. But what could be so special about that date? Kip wondered.

"Sheridan?"

Kip looked toward the door where Miss Feldspar now stood jangling her keys. He'd been so caught up in his thoughts that he hadn't noticed the classroom had emptied.

"Woolgathering?" the teacher asked as he picked up his books and headed for the door.

"Huh? Oh, I was just trying to figure something out.

Miss Feldspar, can you think of anything special about June twenty-first?''

"June twenty-first?" The teacher looked at him oddly, worry suddenly crossing her face. Then just as suddenly the worried look passed and she said, "You mean you've forgotten?"

"Forgotten what?" So it *did* mean something, Kip thought to himself.

"If there's one thing I'd expect you to remember, it's the last day of school." She smiled.

"Oh, right." Kip flushed as he edged by her, doubting that that was what the numbers referred to. He stopped at his locker, then headed outside and found Theo waiting by the bicycle rack. She was straddling a clunky one-speed with a basket on the front.

"How'd it go after I left?" Kip asked, unlocking the chain from his bike and pulling up beside her.

"Vicky left the island this morning."

"Because of us?" Kip asked, incredulous.

"We were just the excuse. She never wanted to come here in the first place."

"What about you and your dad? Are you going to have to leave?"

"I'm not sure. Dad was just waking up when I left. Vicky made him sleep on the living-room couch. But I think we might stay, for a little while anyway. Dad usually likes to give her some time to cool down. I guess her fan-club appearance was a disaster. Dad said no one there really knew much about the show. Not even the Amontis, and they were the ones who organized the whole thing. Dad thinks that's what really set her off.

He said Vicky thought the fan club here was a sham, just a bunch of crackpots who wanted to meet a star. Any star. He said she could hardly stand to be in the same room with the Amontis by the end of the night."

"How did *he* feel?"

"I'm not sure. I think he finds the Amontis a little peculiar. There *is* something odd about them. When I was talking to Aron —"

"Aron?" Kip interrupted, surprised. "How do you know Aron?"

"He was at the restaurant that night. All he talked about was how Marenack and more and more tourists were going to mess up the island. He sure knows a lot about it."

"I'm surprised you got him to talk at all. Whenever I see him, he shuts up like a clam. Say, that reminds me. What restaurant was it?"

"Gone Fishing, or something like that."

"Did you hear they had a fire last night?" Kip asked.

"No. No, I didn't." But Theo had an eerie sense that she *had* known about it somehow.

"Burned right to the ground. The whole thing's floating in the harbor now."

"Do you know how it happened?"

"They're not sure yet, but it's all everyone talked about in school today. At least they all got out in time. I don't think anyone was hurt. Hey, we'd better get moving. The Historical Society's only open till four."

Theo followed as Kip pedaled out of the lot. Vaguely she began to remember a dream, a dream about fire and a boy. It made her uneasy, hearing there'd really been a fire. She coasted along beside Kip to the bottom of Atlantic Avenue. As they turned down the road to town, she felt a damp chill sweep over her, raising goose-bumps on her arms. But there wasn't a breeze, and the sun was beating down. She sensed, more than saw, some movement on the hill to her left. Glancing up, she glimpsed a skeletal hand reaching down at her from above the trees. Losing control of her bike she bumped into the curb, but caught herself by throwing out her feet. Standing on firm ground and drawing her breath, she turned. The great gray slatted arm of the old wind-mill grazed the sky. The *windmill,* Theo thought to her-self, feeling suddenly giddy. But why had it looked that way? And what had given her that terrible chill?

"Hey, hurry up!" Kip called back. Theo pushed away from the curb and pedaled down the street, the arm of the windmill creaking and swaying behind her.

Theo chained her bike by the pillars of the Nantucket Historical Society and followed Kip in through a long, narrow entryway. Their footsteps echoed behind them as they approached a room at the end, where a young woman was reading at a desk. The room was silent as a tomb, with whaling displays along the walls and in a dozen dusty glass cases. There was a damp, musty odor to the air.

Kip approached the woman at the desk. "Miss Pocket?"

"Miss Pocket stepped out, won't be back for another half-hour," the woman answered, fingering the cover of her book, clearly wanting to get on with her reading.

Theo began to feel strangely uneasy. She found the dark, musty room depressing and again had the peculiar feeling that she was being watched. Glancing up, she saw the thirty-foot skeleton of a whale suspended from the ceiling. The enormous, shadowy eye sockets peered down at her.

"We want to find out the meaning of an Indian symbol. Nantucket Indian," Kip told the woman.

"I don't believe we have anything that precedes colonial history in our reading room."

"Where's the reading room?" Kip asked.

"Through the arch." She pointed. Kip started toward it. "But you can't go in alone. Miss Pocket has a strict rule against allowing anyone to use the library unsupervised. I'd help you, but I've got to be in here to answer questions about the exhibits."

Answer what questions? There was no one else there, Kip thought to himself with annoyance.

"Why don't you come back in an hour?" The woman picked up her book.

"But the sign says you close at four. If we come back in an hour, there won't be anyone here," Kip protested. "Couldn't we look it up ourselves? If you tell us how, we'll be very careful."

"I really don't think we have what you're looking for," the woman replied.

"But it's the *Historical* Society!" Kip argued. "There *has* to be something here about the Indians!"

Theo tugged his arm. "Come on, Kip. We'll come back another time."

"Why should we come back when we're already

here?'' Kip sounded aggravated. ''Come on, lady, please?'' he persisted. ''We're not going to hurt anything.''

''I can't bend rules.'' The woman sighed impatiently. ''Miss Pocket would have my scalp if she knew I let you in there unsupervised. We've had trouble with vandals in the past, so she's very fussy about it. Many of those books are irreplaceable.'' She turned at the sound of the outside door swinging open. A large group of tourists were on their way in, looking as though they had just gotten off the boat, with their cameras and picnic hampers.

''Come on.'' Theo nudged Kip. ''Let's look at these whaling displays.'' As she pulled Kip away, the woman eyed them suspiciously.

Soon, more tourists came and the room was filled, many of the people crowding around the woman's desk to ask questions. Unnoticed in the crowd, Theo and Kip moved quickly down the vaulted hall and through the archway. Turning the corner, they entered the reading room, a long room crammed with books from floor to ceiling. At least it had two small windows set high above the shelves, making it warmer and brighter than the room they'd just left, Theo thought to herself.

''Most of it's whaling stuff,'' Kip remarked as he looked over the bookcases.

''Wait, what's that?'' Theo pointed to the topmost shelf in one corner. It was labeled ''Pre-Colonial 1659.''

Kip pulled a ladder, which was suspended on coasters, alongside the shelf where Theo was standing, then climbed it. While peering over the spines of the books at the top, he spotted what looked like a notebook wedged behind the others. He pulled it out.

"It's the only thing up here about Indians," he said after a moment and handed it down.

"Legends and Lore of the Four Nantucket Tribes," Theo read from the cover of the loosely bound journal covered with dust. While Kip climbed down, she sat at a reading table and blew the dust off the cover. "Doesn't look like this one gets read too often," she said. Opening it, Theo saw that it wasn't a printed book but rather a collection of typed sheets held together in a looseleaf binding. "Hey, Kip, look at this!" Beneath the title on the front page was printed: "Compiled by Hester Sheridan from the journals of Marcel DuLac."

"That's Gram!" Kip said with surprise as he pulled up the chair next to her.

Turning the page, Theo read the short preface aloud:

" 'The four Nantucket tribes had an oral tradition, with one family from each tribe carrying forward the history of their people through stories passed down from one generation to the next. These families were called the Memory Keepers, and held the position of highest honor within a tribe, for without a past, they believed their race had no future. But tribal memory was not enough to preserve their race, as time has borne out. The last of the Nantucket tribes vanished by the dawn of the eighteenth century. Their decline began with the arrival of the first colonial settlement in 1659.' "

Theo turned to the table of contents and ran her finger down the page. "I think this is what we want. An index of Indian symbols."

Kip pulled out Gram's list of symbols as Theo turned to the section.

" 'Few symbols were actually used by the Indians,' " Theo read from the introduction above the key. " 'The following collection was taken mostly from paintings on hides and carvings. Most represent what they appear to be, such as wavy lines for water, a branched stick for trees, and so on. Others are totems representing spirits or elements related to a tribe. Combinations of symbols were frequently used to represent a particular place, such as a manito's position of power.' "

"What's a manito?" Kip asked.

"The contents said there's a glossary in the back." Theo marked her place and flipped to the word list at the end of the book. Finding the definition, she read, " 'Each of the four Nantucket tribes was thought to have sprung from one of the elements: Earth, Water, Wind, or Fire. In turn, every member of a tribe was thought to possess the spirit of his tribe's element. The Memory Keepers, who came from the tribes' oldest families, were believed to possess such a high degree of this spirit that they could control the element, as in calming turbulent waters or conjuring winds to bring down the rains for their crops. But to exercise this power they first had to shapeshift to a creature of their element. In these shapeshifted forms, they were referred to as manitos.' "

"Let me see the book," Kip asked, pulling up his chair. "I want to look up that word, *shapeshifted*." Turning further through the glossary, he found *shapeshifting* and read, " 'The art of changing one's form, practiced by Memory Keepers. The Wind tribe appeared as loons in their manito form, the Earth tribe as serpents, the Water people as crabs, and the Fire people as kesaraks.' '' Kip looked down the page to *kesarak* and read, '' 'The manito of Fire appears as a kesarak; a winged, fire-breathing creature with the head and body of a goat, a serpent's tail, and claws. It is the strongest manito, and it represents the strongest element. The kesarak was thought to take its power from the sun, and the loon, crab, and serpent, in turn, took their power from the kesarak. This was consistent with tribal belief that Fire is the origin of all things, also evidenced by tribal drawings which place the kesarak at the center of a ring formed by the other three manitos. This formation was referred to as the Configuration of Unified Power, when all four manitos joined together to exercise their highest power over the elements for a common purpose. The Configuration could only take place once a year, during summer solstice, when the sun is in its strongest position to the earth.' ''

"This stuff is *wild!*" Kip interjected. "People moving around the elements and changing their shapes, like wizards or something." Kip glanced at Theo, who seemed to be deep in thought. The air in the room suddenly felt warm and heavy. Kip absently brushed the back of his hand over the perspiration now beading on his brow. "We still haven't looked up the symbol on your pendant or these things on Gram's paper," he said.

As Kip turned back to the list of symbols, Theo seemed to be staring at the dust swirling up from the table in a fading shaft of sunlight. But her eyes were glazed, and what Kip had mistaken for a thoughtful look was really more like the look of someone dazed.

"Hey," Kip exclaimed, caught up in his own excitement. "These are all the manitos with the symbols for their positions of power. That thing on Altar Rock is the loon. Wait a minute." Kip flipped back to the glossary and read, " 'The loon, a large black bird, is the manito of the Wind tribe.' "

A crackling sound came from directly above. Kip glanced up at the window, where rain had begun to spatter against the glass. "Looks like a storm. Funny, it didn't seem cloudy at all when we came in." Kip could hear the tourists down the hall beginning to leave. He shrugged and turned back to the book. "Hey, guess what? That thing on your pendant is the sign of the kesarak, that goat thing that breathes fire. And it says here its position of power is somewhere in Hidden Forest. And get this. All the positions of power are burial grounds, and that's what makes them powerful, because of the spirits of the people buried there."

Theo still looked lost in thought. Kip held the book toward her, then dropped it on the table at the sudden sound of the outside door slamming shut. A strong wind rushed into the room and flapped the pages of the book. As Kip began to turn back to his place, he heard a thump behind him. Glancing over his shoulder, he was startled to see a tall, gaunt woman with raven-black hair standing by the window at the other end of the room. At the same moment, the clatter of heels echoed from down the hall.

The woman they'd met at the front desk came stalking

into the room. "I *thought* I heard voices down he——"
She caught herself abruptly when she spotted the other
woman. "Miss Pocket." She sounded nervous. "I
didn't see you come in."

"How could you?" Miss Pocket said flatly. "With
your nose always stuck in a book." Then she waved a
hand at the woman as though she were shooing away a
fly. As the woman scurried away, Miss Pocket crossed
the room.

"You were going to read about shapeshifting?"
Theo's voice came softly from the end of the table. She
seemed unaware of Miss Pocket's presence.

"I already did," Kip answered, looking at her curi-
ously.

"I guess my mind must have wandered." Theo
rubbed her eyes. "Is it raining?"

"Didn't you hear the thunder?" Kip asked, leaving the book on the table. "It was so close it practically
shook the room." He noticed that Miss Pocket was
drenching wet and was staring at Theo intently.

Theo glanced up at the window. Perhaps she'd dozed
off and the thunder had awakened her, she thought as
she watched a dim shaft of sunlight begin to filter
through the glass. The flash storm was moving away.
Theo slumped drowsily in her chair. Why did she feel
so tired? she wondered.

"What are you doing with that book?" Miss Pocket
finally spoke to them, sounding grave.

"Looking up a symbol on her pendant," Kip answered. "It's Indian. Someone gave it to her, and we're
trying to find out what it means."

A worried look passed over the woman's face. "So, what did you find?"

"It's the sign for someone with special powers, like the ability to change shape and control the elements," Kip replied.

"*That* old legend." Miss Pocket laughed lightly. "All those old Indian myths are like fairy tales." She picked the book up from the table, carried it to a small, cluttered desk in the corner, and sat down. "I'll put it back. I'm afraid you'll have to leave, we're closing now." She opened a file on her desk and began to write something down.

Theo seemed fully awake now. She pushed herself from the chair. Miss Pocket paid no more attention to them as Theo followed Kip back down the hall to the room with the whaling displays. Theo had the nagging feeling she'd seen Miss Pocket before. Then she realized that the woman was Norma Pocket's sister. *That* was why she looked familiar.

As they approached the entry, a heavyset man in a gray suit came in. He stopped to brush the rain from his shoulders. "That's the principal of my school," Kip whispered to Theo. Mr. Hogarth started up the vaulted hall, hunched a bit and walking stiffly like a man in armor.

"Hello, Mr. Hogarth," Kip greeted the man as he passed.

"Uh . . . hello," Mr. Hogarth replied, looking askance at Theo and not even glancing at Kip.

For a moment, as she watched the man walk away, Theo felt she'd seen him before, too. She recognized his massive gray bulk and jerking gait from somewhere, and his eyes, or the way he looked at her, seemed somehow familiar, too. "I don't know what happened to me in there," Theo remarked. "I feel like I've been asleep for hours."

As they headed down the steps toward their bikes, the horn of a departing ferry sounded from across the harbor. A throng of new arrivals milled over the sidewalks and spilled into the puddled streets. A man with a suitcase in each hand jostled Theo, crowding her off the curb.

"Still like to see the moors?" Kip tossed the chain in his basket and kicked up the kickstand.

"Any place away from here. I can't stand these crowds." Theo straddled her bike and pushed it out to the street, then weaved through the tourists, keeping up with Kip. As they neared the outskirts of town, the dark, drowsy feeling she'd had vanished completely. Already the blazing sun had dried the pavement.

13 Song of the Loon

Kip took Theo up above the town of Nantucket, past the windmill whose sails creaked against their locks with the gentle breeze. They coasted past Kip's school to 'Sconset Road. Theo's bike was hard to pedal once they turned onto the road through the moors, so they walked together over the Shawkemo Hills. At Altar

Rock, they leaned their bikes against the base of the rock and climbed to the top.

"It's hard to imagine there are people buried under here," Kip said thoughtfully, as he sat down at one edge.

"You can practically see forever!" Theo whirled around, scanning the low rolling hills. "What's that?" She pointed across the moors at a distant clump of green.

"Hidden Forest."

"But it looks like a bunch of bushes. Did it get cut down?"

"It's a forest, all right. From here you only see the tops of the trees. The hills hide the rest of it." Kip took out Gram's sheet of paper with the symbols and flatened it over the stone. "Yup, it's exact," he said to himself.

"What's that?" Theo knelt beside him.

"Gram's paper. It's a map. See, all the positions of power line up with the places I read about in the book. The serpent's position is Harp of the Winds, a marshy place over that way." He pointed. "And the crab's position is Sachacha Pond, over in that direction. The way Gram has the symbols arranged is exactly the same as where the real places are. I wonder what she was doing with it?" Kip sprawled across the rock beside Theo and squinted up at the sun. "Imagine those Indians really believing that a person could change shape."

"Maybe they just dressed up like animals." Theo stretched out on the rock beside him. "Although I don't see how someone could dress up like a crab."

"Or a snake," Kip said with a chuckle. "Unless they

were really skinny. It makes me think of stories about werewolves and vampires."

"Do you think all that stuff in the book is just a myth, about changing into goats and birds and conjuring the wind?" Theo asked.

"Of course. Don't you?" Kip leaned on his side and grinned at her. He noticed that Theo's skin was already a deep earthy brown, while his own had only grown pinker and more crowded with freckles. "Hey." He nudged her. "Come on. It's like the librarian said. All that stuff is like a fairy tale."

"I suppose." Theo gazed thoughtfully across the moors. The legend disturbed her. While she'd been riding out to the moors and she'd listened to Kip go over what she had missed when he read from the book, it had all begun to sound familiar, like the Indian names on the map.

Kip stretched and yawned, then pushed himself up. "I'm going to fall asleep if we stay out here much longer. That sun's awfully hot, maybe we should go swim——" He cut himself off as an eerie laugh rolled over the moors. "I've heard that before. The last time I was here." He listened for a moment, but the laugh had gone, and with it the humming of thousands of insects beneath the surrounding shrubs. The moors had become still so suddenly that he could hear the sound of Theo's breathing. She stood beside him, slowly turning her head as she searched the hills.

"Let's ride back." Kip slid from the rock, feeling suddenly uneasy. The sun beating down had now become an unpleasant, scorching glare. "Coming?" He squinted up at Theo, still standing on the rock. At a glance she seemed like no more than an extension of the stone, rigid with her gaze fixed on Hidden Forest. Kip called again, but she didn't turn. Her ears were filled with an echo of laughter reverberating back through time, and the forest across the moors seemed to shrink and grow younger. It turned bare, then green, then exploded with color, as if the seasons of centuries flew by in reverse. The hills around the valley grew softer, rolling like waves with wheat the color of fire. Then a figure walked up from the valley and began wandering through the wheat. It was a dark-skinned woman with long black hair flowing out over her shoulders and fluttering in the wind like a silken shawl. When she raised her face toward the sun, Theo thought for a moment that she was her mother. But this woman was taller and broader, her features more boldly set.

A tiny hand struggled free from a bundle tied to the woman's back. It was a baby's hand, playing with her hair. The woman seemed not to notice, but glanced around as though she were searching for something. Then her eyes met Theo's. She smiled and called her by name. It did not sound like the name Theo's parents had given her, but Theo knew it was hers, and started toward the woman waving in the field. On her second step forward, the world abruptly turned upside down and Theo found herself staring into the sun.

"What are you trying to do? Break your neck?" Kip knelt beside her where he'd pulled her down to the rock. "You almost walked over the edge."

Theo's whole body trembled. The sunlight forced tears

from her eyes. "I . . . I . . ." Theo faltered, wiping the tears from her face. Where was the woman, the fields of wheat? Am I going crazy? she wondered, glancing back at the rocky moors and the green of the forest. "I felt dizzy," she finally answered. Why couldn't she tell him? What made her afraid?

Even through the tan her face seemed paler, Kip thought. "It's probably the sun. It's awfully hot." He held her hand as she slid down the rock.

"Did . . . did you hear a laugh?" she asked, tentative, afraid of what he'd think.

"Yes, and it sounded like a maniac." Kip slid down beside her. "Or some joker trying to scare us. Hey, are you sure you're all right?"

"Did you . . . see anyone?" Theo asked, leaning against the rock.

"Huh?" Kip turned his head around to look over the moors once more. "You mean whoever made that sound? No, but I think it came from the forest, and I'll bet it's someone pulling a prank. That laugh was much too creepy to be for real. Hey, are you sure you're O.K.?" Kip saw that she was shaking.

"It's the sun, that's all. I feel a little lightheaded," Theo said, trying to control her trembling. What had happened? Why had she seen these things? she wondered anxiously. Slowly she pushed her bike back down the path.

When they got to the road Theo pedaled ahead, lost in thought. There on Altar Rock she'd had the same sensation she'd felt in the restaurant just before she blacked out. Like being caught in an undertow, she thought, only she had been pulled down by something deep inside herself, drawn away into a world of nightmares where rooms filled with fire or were buried underwater, where time seemed to leap ahead, or back, and where a person walking toward her could vanish with the blink of an eye. Is this what it meant to go crazy? she wondered. Having nightmares when you're awake?

Theo thought back to the windmill, how it had looked for an instant like a skeletal hand, and then she remembered her first day on the island, when she'd seen the wall of water. Where did these visions come from? she wondered. And why the terrible dreams? She wished she could tell someone — Kip or her father — but she knew they would think it was all in her head. Feeling miserable, Theo let this thought sink in. It's *not* in my head, she told herself. She squeezed her eyes tight to keep from crying. Whatever it was, she knew she would have to figure it out on her own. If she told anyone, they'd just think she *was* crazy, and things were bad enough as they were.

When they reached the shoreline drive, Kip pedaled up beside her. "Want to go for a swim?" he asked.

"No . . . no, I better be getting home. Maybe tomorrow." Theo said goodbye at the top of Kip's drive, then rode on alone.

Back on the moors, a great black bird sailed out of Hidden Forest and circled above the hills. A deep laugh poured from its beak and echoed across the sky. Down below, crickets stopped still in the grass and terns fluttered back to their nests. Peep frogs and turtles slid into the ponds and small downy rabbits darted for their warrens.

The bird swooped down to Altar Rock and perched where Theo had stood. Its sharp eye measured the distance between the sun and the horizon, and then it glanced down at the long, narrow shadow the rock cast back toward the forest. Each day it was growing longer. By solstice, the shadow would touch the trees.

14 The Darkening

Slinging his book bag on the back of a chair, Kip peered over his grandmother's shoulder. The puzzle was nearly complete, with only a few sky pieces left. He studied them, then picked one up and pushed it in place.

"How come you're back so late?" his mother asked on her way through the hall.

"I went to the Historical Society to find out what those symbols meant. And guess what? The book we looked them up in was written by Gram," Kip said proudly. "It was a book about Indian legends. Did you know Gram wrote a book?"

"It was what Gram was working on when she had her stroke." Kip's mother turned down the flame beneath a pot on the stove. "It's not a real book, Kip. It hasn't been published. It's only used as a library supplement." Mrs. Sheridan began setting the table. "So, what did you find out?"

"They're symbols for something called manitos, people who can change their shape and move the elements."

"So *that's* it." Mrs. Sheridan looked up. "That's what she's been trying to say. 'Man two.' She means manito, of course. It's been so long, I'd forgotten."

"But why would she be saying that?" Kip asked.

"Finding that piece of paper must have jarred her memory. It's the last thing she was working on, the old Witch Wood legend."

"The what?" Kip asked.

"An old Indian myth."

Kip frowned. "How come no one ever told *me* about the Indians?"

"I wonder if she was trying to answer you?" Mrs. Sheridan said thoughtfully, gazing at Gram. "Maybe she understands more than we thought."

Kip tugged at his mother's sleeve. "Hey, Mom, how come she never told *me?*"

"I'll talk to you about it later. There's your father."

Kip's ears pricked at the sound of the pickup pulling into the gravel drive. A moment later Mr. Sheridan came through the screen door, looking tired and a bit out of sorts.

"Kip, would you take Gram's puzzle into the other room so I can finish setting the table?" Mrs. Sheridan asked, glancing at her husband with concern. "Bad day?" she asked as Kip started from the room carrying the puzzle board.

"Wasted day." Mr. Sheridan frowned, taking a seat next to Gram. "Hardy keeps stalling on that plane to measure the ground pull. I just can't figure why. He knows how important it is."

"Any new readings on the seismograph?" Mrs. Sheridan brushed the hair back from his brow, then let her hand rest on his shoulder.

"Two." He felt her stiffen. "But they were very weak," he added. His stomach rumbled from hunger and he grinned up at her. "About that strong, and if we don't eat soon, *I'm* going to quake. Had to wait so long at the Coast Guard station I didn't catch a bite to eat."

Kip returned and took the seat across from his father. "Hey, Dad, how come nobody ever told me about any of the old Indian legends?"

"Kip," Mrs. Sheridan interrupted, "I said I'd talk to you about it later."

Mr. Sheridan looked at her questioningly.

"He was at the Historical Society today. He found her collection of legends," Mrs. Sheridan explained.

"How come she never told me about them?" Kip asked.

"Kip, you're like a drip of water." His mother frowned.

His father glanced across at Gram, who fidgeted absently with her napkin. "We asked her not to," he answered.

"Why?" Kip asked with disappointment.

"You were younger then. We didn't want to frighten you," his father replied.

"*Frighten* me. Why would they frighten me? I'd know they were only stories," Kip protested.

"Sometimes Gram didn't."

Then Kip caught the sadness in his father's eyes. "You mean Gram believed them?" he asked with disbelief.

"Gram had been under a terrible strain that year before the stroke. There were cutbacks in the town budget, and funding for the Society was scarce. At one point it almost had to close. Then some journals kept by some colonist turned up."

"The DuLac journals?" Kip asked.

"Yes. Someone found them in the attic of one of the island's old estates. They donated them to the Society. It seems the journals had quite a bit of information about the island's tribes. Up till then so little was known. Then Gram had a brainstorm. The journals were barely decipherable, written by hand in an archaic form of English. Gram figured since nothing had been written about the Indians, a book about them might generate some income to keep the Society going. Most of that last year all she did was work on the book. She began to get obsessed."

"Obsessed?" Kip asked.

"About the legends. It got so that was all she ever thought about. I don't remember just when it started, but after she'd been working on the book for a while, she began to act a bit strange. First she was worried that someone was trying to steal the journals. There was a break-in at the Society, some things were messed up but nothing was taken. But Gram got it in her head for some reason that that was what they were after. I guess the desk where she usually kept them was one of the things the vandals went through. But she had brought them home to work on the night of the break-in, and after that she always kept them with her." Mr. Sheridan glanced at his wife. "Not too long after that," he continued, "Gram began to forget things; just little things here and there, but she imagined it had something to do with the legends. I remember, she called it the Darkening. It had something to do with Indians stealing minds from people who were asleep. By standing in their shadows, I think. Of course, she was just getting senile. People often grow more forgetful as they get older. But Gram insisted it had something to do with the Darkening. Soon after, she had her stroke. When Adele Pocket took over Gram's job running the Historical Society, we gave her Gram's journal. We felt it belonged there. Unfortunately, Gram never did finish transcribing DuLac's original. When we returned it, Adele said she'd try to finish it for her."

Kip tried to remember if Gram had seemed strange back then, but to him Gram had always just been Gram.

"How did you happen to come across Gram's book?" his father asked.

"I went to the Historical Society to look up the symbols on this piece of paper Gram had." Kip pulled it from his pocket. "I found out it's the symbols for the manitos. And Theo has a pendant with the kesarak symbol on it."

"The kesarak, that's from the old Witch Wood legend," his father said thoughtfully.

"What is this Witch Wood legend?" Kip asked.

"Witch Wood was just another name for Hidden Forest," his father answered. "The colonists gave it that name. The forest was sacred, a burial ground, and the squaw called the kesarak manito supposedly lived there. There was some nasty business involving the kesarak and some of the settlers. Gram was very keen on the story. There was something about a lost child, and she even went so far as to look up the genealogies of the people involved."

"What's genealogies?" Kip asked.

"Family trees. There are volumes of them at the Society. They're used to trace the ancestry of the older families on the island. Some go back to the very first settlement. That was another of Gram's obsessions — finding the descendants of the people in these legends."

"You mean she found descendants of some of the Indians? I thought in her book she said they all disappeared."

"Disappeared, Kip, not died. Some of the Indians intermarried and became assimilated into the colony. Like that man who wrote the journals, DuLac, who married an Indian woman. The names of all their descendants are recorded in those books."

"You mean there are people on the island now with Indian blood?" Kip asked excitedly.

Mr. Sheridan nodded, but with an expression that suggested he did not want to discuss the matter.

"Who? Do we know them?" Kip glanced from his father to his mother and back. His parents looked at one another. "Why won't you tell me? Is it some sort of secret?" Kip asked with frustration.

"I'm sure they don't want to be reminded," his

father answered at last. "Gram made it very uncomfortable for them. She thought . . . well, she imagined some rather prominent people on the island were working some Indian magic. It was very embarrassing for everyone concerned. She'd taken to spying on particular individuals and accusing some people outright. She was very bad just before the stroke. It's better left alone."

"Come on, Dad, I won't tell anyone," Kip pleaded.

"No, sport. It was a very unpleasant time for us all. It's better left alone."

"Darn it." Kip sulked. "What about that Witch Wood legend? Will you at least tell me about that?"

"Can't see what harm it would do," Mrs. Sheridan said as she began to serve the meal. "If we don't tell him, he'll just go look it up in that book."

His father sighed. "All right. But after I tell you, I want you to drop all this Indian stuff. Is it a deal?"

"But why?" Kip asked. "It's interesting."

"I don't want you filling your head with these legends the way your grandmother did."

"Oh, all right." Kip nodded grudgingly.

As soon as Mrs. Sheridan sat down, Kip's father began. "The first few years after the colonists arrived they were plagued with bad luck. These settlers were a superstitious lot, and they thought the Indians were working their magic to drive them away. Of course, the Indians had good reason to, since the settlers had invaded their land. But they couldn't have done the things the settlers were accusing them of."

"How do you know they couldn't?" Kip asked. "What sort of things did they accuse them of?"

"Oh, things like causing the earth to spit out their seeds to make the crops fail, or driving their boats into the reefs and chasing the fish from their nets. Of course birds probably ate their seeds and they simply didn't understand the currents around the island, or where the shoals were for good fishing. But a few of the men from the settlement took things into their own hands. They'd heard about the manito myth, and that one manito gave power to the others, so they decided they'd put an end to the Indians' magic by destroying the kesarak. They went to the forest one night, killed her husband, and drowned her in a well."

"They drowned her just because some birds ate their seeds and they didn't know how to fish?" Kip asked.

"Sort of makes you wonder who the real savages were," his father replied.

"They didn't kill the child," Mrs. Sheridan put in. "You at least have to give them that."

"Yes, her child was taken from the island and brought up by a family on the mainland. It was the last of the kesarak's line, and they believed that with the child gone the Indians could work no more magic. After that, there were stories about the ghost of the squaw. Supposedly she roamed the moors in search of her child, and some settlers thought she lured people back to her well to drown them in revenge. Apparently, for years after, whenever someone disappeared they'd pin it on the ghost of the squaw who drowned in Witch Wood."

"Was there anything about the ghost laughing?" Kip asked. "Were there any legends about that?"

"Laughing? No, I don't think so. Why?"

"I've been hearing this weird laugh on the moors, and when I look —"

"Oh, Kip!" Mrs. Sheridan cut him off. "Honestly, George, you should never have told him."

"You *told* me to tell him," Mr. Sheridan replied.

"You know there's no such thing as ghosts," Kip's mother said firmly. "So don't you start in, Kip. It was bad enough with Gram."

"Poor Gram." Mr. Sheridan reached across the table and patted Gram's hand. For a fraction of a second her hand trembled slightly. Kip's father squeezed it, thinking the shaking was the unsteadiness of old age.

When the trembling passed, the greenheads began to buzz with a fury against the screen. Kip glanced at the door, wondering what had set them off.

Mr. Benedict's voice, as he talked on the hall phone, was low and strained. Theo, nestled in a corner of the living room couch, listened while staring at the book in her lap. She had stared at the same page for close to an hour, unable to stop thinking about what she'd seen on the moors. But hearing her father's voice she forgot herself, and when he came into the room she saw the pain in his face. He wouldn't want to talk about it, but all the same she knew how Vicky had hurt him. She couldn't tell him about the visions now. Vicky . . . how could anyone be so self-centered, so cruel? Theo thought. Then a wave of anger rippled through her, ringing in her ears like laughter.

Mr. Benedict glanced up at the tinkling crystal chandelier suspended above the couch. He crossed the room, closed the deck doors against the wind, then began to fix himself a drink. Theo seemed engrossed in her book again when he sat down beside her. He thought he heard a faint buzz in the air and glanced up, looking for a fly. Again the chandelier tinkled lightly. He glanced at it, shrugged, then picked up the paper and began to read.

Outside, the sand whipped up from the dunes and swept around the house. The surf churned and the fog crept in. Theo stared at her book, unseeing.

Across the island, behind a house off Eel Point Road, Aron Amonti walked with his mother along the pebbly shore.

"Your father's afraid Hester Sheridan may be regaining her memory," his mother said worriedly. "With all our energies turned on the girl, it's harder to block Hester's past."

Aron stopped with his mother at the edge of the water, looked down at the swirling foam and then out at the sea. A low, thick fog rolled slowly toward them, riding the incoming tide.

"It's building much too fast, Aron. The fire went well as a trial, but Miss Pocket said a storm broke out today when she approached the girl. There's more anger in her than any of us anticipated. Not just that of the race but an anger of her own. Your father suspected this after the shifting winds the very first day. The next day, the broken glass showed the aimlessness of her anger. Unless we're near to direct it, it could become dangerous. And her sight has Hogarth worried. He watches her sleep, but the visions grow stronger. It's becoming much harder to block her.''

She shuddered, then turned to face Aron. ''Her anger has crossed her power again! Did you feel it?''

Aron nodded, sensing the faint, disturbed feeling in the air that marked the slight tremor. The distant moans of the Sankaty Head and Great Point foghorns sounded. Beams from the island's three lighthouses swept the sea.

Aron's mother touched his arm. ''The earth is restless. It will be better if we sleep.''

Aron followed her back across the sand. The sweeping beam from the Brant Point lighthouse poured over their tracks, illuminating several glistening black scales scattered among their footprints.

15 The Well in Witch Wood

Flames crept over the doorsill and onto the carpet, then leapt to the walls and burned their way toward the bed. Theo lay in terror, unable to breathe, to move, or to shout. The fire crackled across the ceiling, and a moment later the sagging beams snapped.

Theo's eyes blinked open and she shuddered with relief: There was no fire, and the beams stretched straight and sturdy above her. The nightmares had come back, she fretted. Where did they come from? What did they mean? Theo pulled her blanket up against the damp, chilly air. She squinted through the gray at the clock by her bed. Seven-thirty. She did not want to go back to sleep. She might dream again. Shivering, she reached for the robe draped over the bedpost and slipped it on. Sheets of rain poured down outside her window, and beyond, the morning fog hung like a shroud above the dunes. Theo flicked on the light and started down the hall.

The tiles on the bathroom floor felt like ice beneath her feet. She sat at the edge of the tub and turned on the faucet, letting the warm water splash over her outstretched hand. She shivered, anxious for the tub to fill, and gazed down at the bottom where her reflection stared back up at her like a face caught beneath the water. Theo stiffened as a familiar image leapt into her mind — the image of a street filled with murky red light. Objects and people drifted past, floating, underwater . . . Theo jerked back her hand. Scalding water was pouring from the faucet. Trembling, she turned on the cold to kill the sting. The image of the street was gone, but this time the memory remained. She left the water running and went down the hall to her father's room. She had to tell him, she could no longer keep it inside.

Quietly she opened her father's door. How should she begin? she wondered. What could she say? That with the blink of an eye, fires and floods raged through her mind? Even if she could make him believe her, what good would it do? she thought sadly. How could he help her? Theo treaded softly across the room, then stood and watched him through the darkness.

Mr. Benedict's sheet was in a knot at the foot of his bed. One arm hung down to the floor while the other was buried beneath his pillow. Pages of the *Destiny* script were scattered around the bed. Though he was asleep, one hand still held a pencil. Theo pulled the sheet up over him and gently took the pencil away. She gathered the pages from the floor and stacked them neatly on the night table. Doing these things made her feel safe for the moment. Her hand paused before pulling the chain on the reading lamp. She looked down at him breathing softly, his mouth slack. If he knew she was seeing these things, would he have her put away? she wondered. Isn't that what one does?

Theo put out the light and walked back down the hall. Turning off the water, she slipped into the tub. Cradled in the warmth of the bath, the vision she'd had on the moors returned. She pictured the forest shrinking, growing young, and the hills turning gold with wheat. She recalled the face of the woman who had emerged from the forest. Her mother's face smiling, calling her by an unknown yet familiar name. She remembered feeling drawn to this woman she'd seen. *Seen*, Theo thought to herself. She *had* seen the woman. They had looked at one another. She was *real*.

Theo thought again of the forest and land growing young, as if whisked back through centuries. Could she have been seeing the past? she wondered. Suddenly it seemed to her that this woman she had seen on the moors was the key to the visions. I must go back, Theo thought. If she's real, then I will find her.

On the way to his last class, Kip was surprised to see Theo through the corridor windows. He tried to get her attention, but after she leaned her bike at the rack she crossed the field to sit in the shade of a tree.

The morning rain had cleared, but a clamminess remained in the air. No breeze came through the window, and added to the blazing heat of the sun, the humidity made Kip sluggish.

Through most of Miss Feldspar's class it was all Kip could do just to stay awake. He'd been having trouble concentrating most of the day, and seeing Theo waiting had made it harder. Several times he glanced at the date on the blackboard. Tomorrow was June nineteenth, and two days after was the twenty-first. Why had Gram written that date on the list of symbols? he wondered. Was there some special connection between them?

Kip glanced at the clock and fanned himself as the period neared an end. The class was discussing Anne Frank's *Diary*.

"Why didn't they try to escape? Why would three people deliberately imprison themselves in a tiny room, in the middle of a city that was collapsing all around them?" Miss Feldspar looked toward a raised hand. "Yes, Amy?"

"Because they were afraid?"

"Yes, they were frightened. Who wouldn't be? But why didn't they try to escape? Stacey?"

"It was their home. They were stubborn and wouldn't leave because they loved it and felt they belonged there. And they believed the Allied forces would eventually liberate the city."

"Believed . . ." Miss Feldspar said thoughtfully. "They loved their city and felt they belonged there. But how could they be sure the Allied forces would win? No one could know how the war would end. What was it that kept them there in spite of all adversity? Yes, Aron?"

"Hope." The boy's voice sounded odd. He pronounced the word as if it were a prayer.

"Hope," Miss Feldspar repeated. "Belief in what they thought was right, and unflagging hope that right would prevail. That is what gave them the strength to endure great sacrifice and suffering. I'd like you to read the next twenty pages for tomorrow." Miss Feldspar closed the book. "Class dismissed."

As Kip moved toward the door, he saw that Aron remained at his desk, his hands clasped tightly around his book. Aron was gazing toward the window. His cheeks glistened wetly in the sunlight. Were those tears? Kip wondered. Had the plight of Anne Frank actually moved Aron to tears?

Outside, Kip met Theo by the bike rack. "Hi! What are you doing here?" he asked.

"I was going to ride out to the moors and thought you might want to come along." Throughout the morning, the strange pull Theo felt toward Hidden Forest had grown stronger. But she felt less brave than driven, and she wanted Kip with her.

"Sure. Hey, is everything O.K.?" Theo seemed a bit glum, Kip thought, and there were dark circles under her eyes.

"I'm all right. I didn't sleep too well last night, that's all."

"How come you're not wearing the pendant?" Kip asked, unchaining his bike.

"I forgot it," she replied, but she had deliberately left it behind. It had come to feel heavy and unattractive. With its twisted horns and pointed beard, the symbol of the goat scored deeply in the stone had reminded her of a devil.

"Well, I found out some more about the legends last night. It turns out the kesarak manito, the one on your pendant, was drowned in Hidden Forest."

Kip's words struck Theo like a blow. The kesarak's element was fire, she remembered, the fire raged through the rooms in her dreams. Did the visions of worlds beneath water have something to do with the drowning? Maybe her visions were somehow related to the pendant.

"Ready?" Kip was straddling his bike. Theo pulled out beside him. As they rode to the moors, Kip retold the Witch Wood story. Theo listened intently. If the visions did connect to the pendant, she thought, then maybe, now that she'd taken it off, they would stop. She'd only removed the pendant that morning. If nothing else, this trip to the moors would be a test.

Kip noticed another Marenack sign planted at the edge of the moors. "Damn Marenack's like a fungus," he muttered.

Theo didn't respond but rode silently ahead. When they reached Altar Rock, she kept going.

"Don't you want to stop here?" Kip asked.

"Could we look at Hidden Forest?" Theo stared across the hills toward the wooded valley from which the woman had come.

"Sure, why not?" Kip rode on beside her, wondering at her silence. Perhaps there'd been more trouble at home, he thought. She seemed so gloomy. When the path ended, they walked their bikes over the craggy hills spotted with heather and briers and coarse yellow grass. They stopped together at the crest of the slope that led down to Hidden Forest. Kip looked up at a small plane passing overhead, while Theo stared intently into the woods, not seeming to hear it.

"What's it like in the forest?" Theo asked.

"I don't know. I've never gone farther than this."

"Living here your whole life?" Theo asked with surprise. "Weren't you ever curious?"

"Not really. It's just a small woods. I like the open moors better." Kip squinted after the vanishing plane, its wingtips flashing in the sunlight.

Theo set the kickstand on her bike and started down the slope.

"That's a Coast Guard plane," Kip observed, still following it with his eyes. "You can tell by the insignia under . . . hey!" Glancing down, he saw Theo pushing her way through the undergrowth at the edge of the woods. "Hold up!" he called after her, letting his bike fall to the ground and sliding down the slope. At the bottom he spotted a wooden sign nailed to a tree at the edge of the forest.

PRIVATE PROPERTY — NO TRESPASSING
FOR SALE INFORMATION, CONTACT ORIN HARDY

"Hey, Theo, wait up!" Kip shouted as he ran past it. A few feet into the forest he abruptly stopped. A deep-throated laugh, like an oboe, sounded from above. Little sky was visible through the canopy of leaves. Kip moved slowly ahead through the tangle of saplings and overgrown brush. The forest seemed nearly impenetrable.

"Theo?" he called again, pushing farther in. A strong wind swept through the trees, rustling leaves and creaking branches. Kip would have liked to turn back, but he couldn't leave without Theo. As he moved deeper in, the woods seemed to get darker. The treetops shut out most of the sky, leaving only a few threads of light streaming through to the forest floor.

Somewhere ahead, Kip heard a branch snap. "Theo!" he shouted, then pushed on.

Theo had heard Kip behind her, but she felt compelled to move forward toward the sound of a baby sobbing. As she walked, the sound seemed to shift, from left to right, near to far, until she found herself lost in a tangle of tall, dark trees with gnarled and twisted trunks. The lower branches reached toward her as if to draw her further in.

* * *

Kip stumbled through the brambles and emerged from the forest, thorns and small round burrs clinging to his jeans. The plane he'd spotted earlier now hovered like a fly above Great Point, slowly growing larger as it circled back. The strange, warbling laughter drifted out through the trees, and Kip began to pace along the edge of the forest, calling out Theo's name.

While Theo's ears still strained toward the baby's cries, a mist like a damp and fragrant blue smoke appeared, coiling through roots and streaming out over the ground. The air, the woods, everything seemed to grow thicker as Theo moved deeper into the forest. The trees seemed almost to move, crowding closer like dark and silent men huddling around her, pushing her on.

Shhh . . . shhh, the wind hushed through the branches. Abruptly the hideous laugh rang out just ahead. Theo turned to run but stumbled on a root, grazing her head against a tree trunk as she fell. The forest filled with darkness.

"Theo!" Kip called down a narrow, overgrown path he'd found while circling the woods. Thorny shrubs and branches caught on his clothes as he pushed through the forest, clinging, slowing him down, holding him back.

When Theo's head cleared, she found herself lying on a bed of moss and ferns. She leaned to her side at the sound of footsteps crunching through leaves. Her head ached as she squinted through the darkness. A tree seemed to move. She caught her breath, then saw it was the raven-haired woman with the child on her back, slipping through a tangle of saplings just ahead.

Shhh . . . shhho, the wind whispered. Theo stood to follow the woman, but she had vanished as quickly as she had appeared. The air had grown cold and the trees now looked bare as in winter. A soft, rhythmic beating seemed to come from beneath the ground. Again the sobbing sounded, and a dozen yards ahead Theo glimpsed a broad column of moonlight pouring down through the trees. As she approached it, the trees grew sparse and she found herself near a clearing. With a chill of recognition, Theo saw that it resembled the meadow where the figures in her dreams had stood.

At the opposite edge of the clearing she spotted a shelter fashioned from branches, and against a nearby stump leaned a bow-shaped piece of wood. Theo heard the sound of splashing water, and, turning, she saw the raven-haired woman kneeling by a circle of stones. Mesmerized, Theo watched her unfasten the bundled child from her back, then gently set the infant on the grass beside her. Leaning forward, the woman began to pull something from the ring of stones.

Suddenly, several men in strange clothing rushed from behind a cluster of trees. The ground trembled and again the eerie laughter broke out above. Glancing up, Theo spotted a dark bird swooping down through the branches. A loud splash sounded. Looking back to where the woman had been, Theo now saw only the men. The baby cried as one of them gathered it up in his arms.

Shhh . . . shhh . . . shhho. The wind rushed around Theo. *Shoshawna!* it roared in her ears like a chorus of wailing voices, pulling her forward, pressing her toward the ring of stones in the clearing. With each step she took, the earth shivered as though it were alive. The men moved back, shimmering, fading, and then vanished in thin air. When she reached the ring of stones, Theo found that they circled a well. Looking into it, she saw black hair billowing beneath the water's surface. The water bubbled and swirled, sweeping the hair aside. A downy-muzzled creature with bright red eyes stared up at her.

Theo's hand flew to her mouth, and in horror she saw a claw fly to the creature's face beneath her, as if the water reflected her own movement. When she screamed, the water erupted in flames and Theo reeled. All around the clearing the trees moaned and swayed, and behind them a grinding and whirring sound grew, accompanied by flashes of steel cutting through the leaves. Then the trees came toppling toward her, and the earth trembled so violently it threw her to the ground. As Theo fell, smothering darkness surrounded her.

"Theo!" Kip's voice cut through the darkness like a light.

Theo struggled up, blinking open her eyes. She was lying in the branches with the warm sunlight filtering down through the trees. It sparkled gold a few feet away in a tiny pool of water.

Kip shook her by the shoulder. "What *happened* to you?" He knelt beside her, putting a hand to her brow.

"The ground . . . it, it was shaking." Theo glanced

all around. Scraggly shrubs sprung up everywhere. Kip was hovering over her.

When Kip withdrew his hand from her forehead, there was blood on his fingertips. "You must have hit your head. You're bleeding."

"The ground — it moved." She pushed herself unsteadily to her knees.

"Theo, you must have tripped."

She touched her forehead. It felt sticky.

"Come on." Kip pulled her by by one arm.

"I thought —" she began, then cut herself off. Her eyes had lighted on several jagged pieces of stone partially buried beneath the pine needles. "Wait!" She pulled her arm free and stooped to pick them up.

"What is it?" Kip kneeled by her. "Hey, arrowheads."

"Then I did see it," Theo said softly.

"See what?" Kip asked.

"A bow. There was a stump here, and a bow was leaning against it," she said nervously, still frightened but also relieved to find something from her vision. Slowly she began to explain to Kip about the woman and the name the wind had called, but something kept her from telling him about the face in the water.

"And before she drowned, she set a baby down. I'm almost sure I heard it cry. And the wind called Shoshawna, hush Shoshawna," Theo finished, then watched him hopefully.

Kip touched the dried blood on her forehead. "Theo, it must have been a dream. You were unconscious when

I found you. And it's too much like the Witch Wood story. That's what dreams are all about, just different things we've heard or seen all jumbled together.''

"But the arrowheads? They were right where I saw the bow.''

"Maybe you saw the arrowheads before you fell, then they showed up in your dream. Theo, *I've* even found arrowheads on the moors.''

"Kip, look!'' Theo pointed at the well, which was half concealed by brambles.

From where Kip stood, it looked like no more than a puddle in a ring of black stones. But he followed her to it and helped her push back the briers. "You're right, it is a well. Maybe you saw that, too, before you fell.''

Theo looked around for the remains of the lean-to. There were none.

"Hey, look here!'' Kip crouched by the well. Moss and lichen crept over the rim. He could just make out the horns of the goat symbol etched in the largest stone. "Just like the mark on your pendant,'' he said. "This must be the kesarak's position of power.''

Theo seemed agitated. "And the well where the squaw was drowned,'' she added nervously. "Kip, something brought me here.''

"Look, Theo.'' Kip gestured toward the path. "Even though you can't see it very well, there's some sort of a path leading here. You followed it without even knowing, because it was the easiest way to walk. Come on, let's go back.''

"Wait.'' Theo held his arm firmly, a look of unwavering certainty on her face. "I saw her, Kip. And those men, too. As clear as I see you now. And the name the wind . . ."

"Theo!" Kip's voice came out louder than he had intended. "It's the twentieth century! There are no such things as ghosts! It was all a dream." Kip stared at her till she looked away. "Come on." He touched her arm gently. "We better stick together this time."

Theo let him lead her back through the forest. There was no way she could convince him, she realized. Even if the visions *weren't* in her head, she was the only one who could see them. And these visions were not jumbled versions of things she already knew about. What of the floods and fires? If they were dreams, then why did they come mostly when she was awake?

After they found their way out of the forest, they got their bikes and walked past the cranberry bog to Gibb's Pond. Theo sat while Kip dampened his handkerchief to wipe the blood from her forehead. "You'll probably get a good bump," he said. He shooed a fly and wiped the blood away. His hand jerked when the familiar laugh suddenly sounded from the forest behind them.

"It's the bird," Theo whispered, reaching toward her brow.

"What's that?" Kip asked.

"Nothing," Theo mumbled. The laughter had stopped.

"Come on." Kip tugged her by the arm. "This place is getting to me."

"You're scared, too?" Theo asked.

"No. I'm just sick of listening to that joker. He can laugh his head off, but we don't have to listen. Come on."

At the Institute of Oceanography, Kip's father frowned over the seismograph. He was comparing the markings on the graph to the readings he'd taken from the airplane. The phone on his desk rang.

"Mr. Sheridan, it's Commander Hardy. Could you see me in my office, say, in twenty minutes?"

"Could it wait until morning, sir? I was just about to go out and check the strata between Polpis and the Madequecham. That's the region we were over when we picked up those abnormal gravity readings."

"In twenty minutes, Mr. Sheridan. It's important."

"But I've got to start going over that terrain by foot while it's still daylight. This could be a serious fault and —"

"Hang the fault!" Hardy's voice came angrily over the wire. "I need to talk to you *now*, Sheridan!" The receiver slammed down.

Commander Hardy's office looked out on the head of the harbor. When Kip's father entered, the commander had his back to the door. Smoke drifted up from his cigar as he watched an incoming ferry overflowing at the deck with tourists. "Sit down, Mr. Sheridan," he said without turning.

Kip's father closed the door and took a seat before the commander's desk.

"I hear you made some of our boys pretty nervous today." Smoke coiled over the commander's head like a halo.

"I'm not sure what you mean, sir. If you're referring to the fault —"

"Some of them have this crazy idea that we're sitting on top of a time bomb," the commander interrupted. "Where do you suppose they got that idea?"

"Those men were working with me, sir. I couldn't very well explain what I wanted them to do without telling them why."

"Why not?" the Commander asked coolly, still staring out the window. "I've often sent men out on missions without telling them why. For security reasons."

"This isn't espionage, sir, it's a fault with an active probability factor of —"

"Let me finish," Commander Hardy cut him off. He turned and flipped a manila folder across the desk. "Could you read that back to me, Sheridan?"

Kip's father glanced down at the heavy black letters. "That's the code for classified projects." He looked up, not understanding.

"Glad I don't have to explain it to you. What branch of the service were you in?"

"Navy."

"Navy, good. Then we should work well together." The commander smiled and leaned forward. "From here on, anything you see on the seismograph is to be considered classified. For the time being I'll be supervising your work, so you'll report to me directly. Because you work for a government agency, Sheridan, you realize you are under my jurisdiction in a time of crisis?''

Kip's father was silent. He remembered the maritime code and knew this was true. ''Why?'' he asked after a few moments.

''Because you've created a crisis. But I've had a chat with the boys. They all think it's a false alarm.'' The heavy man leaned forward till Kip's father could smell the smoke on his breath.

''But it's *not* just a false alarm. The expedition bears it out.''

''*You* know that'' — the commander flicked the ash from his cigar to the floor — ''and *I* do, and that's as far as I want this to go, for the time being. Understood?''

''It picked up a one-point-six on the Richter scale at three forty-three. It's gotten much stronger, and if it goes any higher people will start to feel it.''

''If!'' The commander angrily stumped out his cigar. ''You want to start a panic based on an *if?*''

''This could well be a new fault, Commander. It's impossible to tell how great a shift it could cause. I explained all that on the phone. We've been lucky these tremors have been so weak. Usually these things give no warning at all.''

''And what if it never happens? What if we never get anything higher than a two? Didn't you say anything under a two was virtually harmless? That this thing could just go on easing itself into place with these smaller tremors? You told me that was a likely course.''

''I don't believe we should proceed on that assumption, sir. It's too risky, if this thing decides to blow. If we don't prepare people for the worst, the only warning they'd get would be the foreshock, which may only last seconds, a few minutes at most. It's insidious, this thing. Half the time no one even knows when it's begun. Air gets a bit fuzzy, might hear a faint buzz, and maybe you see a little more dust than usual. Then your legs go a little trembly, and by the time you've sat down to figure out what's going on, you might just find your roof caving in.''

Beads of perspiration trickled down the commander's brow. He loosened his tie and ran a finger along the inside of his collar. "Sheridan, I want this kept quiet.''

"But sir, there's no telling how much time we've got, if a bigger one *is* coming.''

"Have you ever been caught in a panic, Sheridan?'' The commander's tone was grave. "Imagine thousands trying to exit this island at once. We don't have enough boats to make a dent, not with the tourist season on us. There'd be people hurt, maybe killed. And think of the looters hanging behind, because the island would *still* be here. We can't afford to create mass hysteria. If there's any preparation, it will be done discreetly, we'll move in an orderly fashion to cause the least alarm possible. I'm working on a plan now, a civil defense evacuation scheme. Keep on top of this thing, but keep it under your hat. I don't want another leak until our plans are ready. Am I understood?''

"Yes, Commander.''

"You'll report any new developments back to me directly. And from here on you'll be working this thing alone.''

"What about a night shift? After today, I think someone ought to be watching twenty-four hours."

"I've screened a few of the new recruits; there's one fellow who ought to function well as a pair of eyes to watch your equipment. He thinks your graph is measuring sea currents." The commander smiled and shook his head. "Where we got *him* from, God only knows. So it's down to you and me, and I want it kept that way."

A voice sounded over the commander's intercom: "Marenack calling, Commander Hardy. Pick up on extension three."

"You can go now, Sheridan." The commander had his hand over the phone. Kip's father nodded and left.

Theo's father made an effort to compose himself before Theo returned. Vicky's call had been brief, but then there wasn't much left to say. The division of property, settlements, and so forth would be handled by their attorneys. It had all come undone as quickly as an episode of *Destiny Jones,* he thought wryly.

He recognized the sound of Theo's bike coming over the gravel. Opening the door, he looked out at the dunes glistening like silver in the sun. Who would have guessed how much this trip to the island would change our lives? he thought sadly.

16 Kindred Spirits

"It's better, really, for all of us." Mr. Bene t was sitting with Theo in the window booth of a restaurant on Main Street. Both were picking disconsolately at their food. "Hey, come on, this dinner ought to be a celebration." He smiled.

Theo nodded and managed to smile in return. She knew he was trying to cheer her up, but her thoughts kept drifting back to Hidden Forest.

"Sorry we have to cut the trip short," he said.

"When are we leaving?"

"Couldn't get us booked on a flight till the day after tomorrow. Sorry, honey. Maybe we can take another trip later in the summer."

"It's all right. I'm ready to go back." If only the nightmares and visions would end when they left the island, she thought hopefully.

"What do you want to do with our last two days here?" her father asked.

Theo shrugged. To be close to him, to feel safe, was all she wanted.

"Maybe we ought to do a little sightseeing. Any interest in visiting the Nantucket Historical Society? Miss Pocket mentioned she had quite a sizable collection of whaling artifacts. I'd like to see some of these things before I leave. I hardly feel like I've been away at all."

"When did you meet Miss Pocket?" Theo's mind flicked back to the present and she straightened in her seat.

"The night Vicky met with the island's Destiny Club. She and her sister were both there. I swear they must have twisted arms to get people to go. I had the distinct impression that hardly anyone there watched the show."

"You told me." Theo slumped back in her booth. For some reason, it struck her as odd that Miss Pocket had been there. She hardly seemed the sort to follow a soap opera.

"Apart from the Amontis," Mr. Benedict went on, "the Pockets and some fellow named Hogarth were the only ones there who asked halfway intelligent questions."

"Mr. Hogarth?" Theo recalled the stiff, bulky man Kip had pointed out at the Historical Society library. He seemed an even less likely fan than Miss Pocket. Theo glanced thoughtfully out the window overlooking the busy street. Tourists streamed in and out of the row of souvenir shops on the opposite side. What had it been about Hogarth? she wondered. Why had he seemed so familiar?

"It was the oddest collection of people, really — all island types, I suppose. But I shouldn't complain. They were very generous, with the Stanhope house and all."

Theo thought of the pendant and of the symbol of the goat, the manito symbol for the woman who had drowned in the well. Apart from the possibility of its connection to the visions, the pendant now seemed an odd gift, considering its significance.

"Theo, isn't that the Amonti boy?" Her father interrupted her thoughts. Following his gaze, she caught sight of Aron beneath a street lamp by the opposite curb. He seemed to be staring right at them.

"Why don't you ask him to join us? I only met him briefly the night of Vicky's appearance. Serious, but he seems a nice enough fellow. Call him over, I can have him tell his parents we're leaving."

But as Theo raised her hand, Aron shrank back in the shadows of an alley across the street. Theo slid from the booth and started for the door. She had another reason for wanting to talk to Aron. She wanted to see what he knew about the pendant. Theo's father watched her cross the street and disappear into the crowd.

Theo pushed her way through the tourists streaming over the sidewalk. An echo of footsteps drifted out of the darkened alley. It had seemed he was looking right at them, she thought. If he'd seen her, why had he hurried away? For a moment her eyes caught a flicker of movement in the shadows at the end of the alley.

"Aron?" she called, but was answered only by footsteps. "Aron, wait!" she shouted. The footsteps faded into a sound like something being dragged across the ground. Theo started into the alley, avoiding the garbage stacked along the walls. Where could he have gone? she wondered. The alley appeared to be a dead end. She was about to turn around when she heard a rubbish can crash to the pavement. "Aron?" she said softly, starting forward again. Something crackled underfoot. Glancing down, she saw she was walking on a trail of shiny black scales. Like the ones she'd found by the Stanhopes', she thought as she followed them to where they disappeared behind an overturned barrel. Then she heard a rustling sound coming from a mound of rubbish at the far end of the alley.

"Aron, is that you?"

A box in the corner shifted slightly, as though something were pushing behind it. Was he trying to hide from her? she wondered. But why? She nudged the box with her toe, squinting into the shadows. A hiss like a cat sounded, then something slid heavily over her foot. Theo jumped back, upsetting more rubbish, and boxes toppled around her. Kicking them aside she ran back to the street.

"Lose him?" her father asked as she sat back down.

Theo nodded, breathless. What *was* that thing in the alley? she wondered. And how had Aron gotten by her?

"It's O.K., I'll call his parents tomorrow to let them know our plans."

I saw him go into that alley, Theo thought, I'm *sure* I did. But how did he get out? Then she thought again of the gift the Amontis had given her. If the pendant was related to the visions, were the Amontis connected to them, too? Her mind jumped forward and backward, from the thing in the alley to the thing in the well, from the pendant to the legend.

"Dad, can we go home? I'm tired." She needed to think, to figure this out. She was close now, she felt, and it scared her.

* * *

After washing the dishes, Mrs. Sheridan went to her husband's study, where she found him poring over an odd-looking map of the island. "What is that, George?" she asked.

"It's what we took the plane up for. It's a record of the gravitational pull at different sites on the island. If there's much variance in the pull of a given area, it might suggest a fault. But it isn't foolproof, and some of these measurements look completely haywire."

"Why, what's wrong?"

"After the first reading, we circled back in the plane and I took a backup measurement. The two readings should have been consistent, unless a substantial quake had occurred when the plane was over these areas. Which there wasn't, or believe me, we'd know about it."

"I don't understand." Mrs. Sheridan leaned over the study table strewn with maps and charts.

"Jinny, these two sets of measurements were taken within forty minutes of each other. We'd have needed a quake big enough to shake this whole island apart to get such a great leap in these measurements over such a short period of time. It's an impossible reading."

"Could there be something wrong with the instruments?"

Mr. Sheridan shrugged. "I don't know what else to think. This reads as if a magnet with pull as great as the North Pole was dragged between these two points. If I didn't know better, I'd say there was an invisible active volcano roaming over the moors."

"The moors?" His wife grew tense. "Is that where

it is? Oh, George, Kip was out there today with that girl from the Stanhope house.''

"Jinny.'' He took her hand, smiling gently. "All these gravity readings tell me is that it's time to buy new equipment. And as far as the seismograph goes, all the tremors have registered under a two. A series of tremors that small can sufficiently ease the tension to avert a major quake. As best I can tell, that's what's happening.'' He did not remember if he'd already told her that such things were utterly unpredictable.

Kip sat at his desk bent over an open dictionary. Above it he had placed Gram's list of symbols. "The loon is distinguished by its song, which sounds like laughter,'' he read. Something Theo had said on the moors, a bare whisper, had taken hold in his mind. The laughter, she'd said, had come from a bird. Why had Theo thought it was a bird? There'd been nothing about laughter in the legend. And besides this, the name Theo thought she'd heard, Shoshawna . . . where had that come from? Could Theo have heard someone speaking in the forest? Something wasn't right, he thought to himself. It just didn't fit. Why would anyone bother to wait and hide in the middle of nowhere just to scare them? And not once but several times? Could someone be trying to scare people away for a reason? And why would they use that eerie laugh? Was it connected to the legend? And if so, how had Theo known about the loon's song? But she hadn't said loon, he reminded himself. All she'd said was bird. Still . . .

Kip's eyes dropped down to the bottom of Gram's

piece of paper. 6–21. What was special about June twenty-first? It had to have something to do with the symbols. Could it have been more than just a coincidence, he wondered, that Gram had turned up these symbols just before the Amontis gave Theo the pendant? And the pendant itself, did the Amontis know what it stood for?

Something was going on. Something, he worried, that had to do with Theo and Gram and this manito legend. Part of the answer was waiting at the Historical Society, he suspected. And if the date had any significance, he'd have to work fast. June twenty-first was only three days away.

As Theo lay in her bed, her mind whirled with questions — about the visions, the legend, the laughter on the moors, the pendant, and finally Aron. Why had he avoided her? And how had he left the alley? Then, recalling the thing sliding over her foot in the darkness, she shuddered.

A sound began to echo in her ear. *Shhh . . . shhh . . .* it lulled her, like a whisper on the wind . . . *Shhh . . . Shoshawna.* Theo's eyelids grew heavy and she relaxed, a wave of velvety darkness washing over her.

Black wings rustled on the roof above, wings that would guide her through sleep.

17 Shadows of Forgotten Ancestors

After school the next day, Kip rode directly to the Historical Society. He had a strong hunch his questions about the pendant, the legend, and the laugh on the moors might be answered, in part, in the genealogies. At least it would be a beginning.

The woman at the desk was busy with tourists. Kip slipped by her unnoticed. The reading room was empty, but the shelf with the genealogies was labeled and Kip quickly found what he was looking for. When he pulled out the volume marked *A* he felt a twinge of guilt for disobeying his father, but soon he lost himself in the search for the Amontis' family tree. Once he found it, he traced his finger up the network of names beginning with Aron's. A dozen generations back, the surname changed to DuLac. Kip's eyes widened as he scanned back to the very first entry. Not only were the Amontis descended from the man who had written the journals but in the position of DuLac's wife was the name Wauwinet of the Earth Tribe. So the Amontis *were* descended from an island tribe. Kip moved his finger back down the page. Odd, he thought, all the men in the line were direct descendants of DuLac and his Indian wife. Why had the name been changed to Amonti? he wondered. Were they trying to hide their ancestry? And the pendant — was it an old family heirloom after all?

Perplexed, Kip reshelved the volume and reached for the one marked *S*. Was it a name on the wind, he wondered, or a name Theo had heard in a half-conscious state, spoken by a flesh-and-blood person? That is, if it was a name at all, he mused as he glanced over the index. Perhaps the Amontis or someone else were digging up treasures from the lost burial grounds. If they were valuable, wouldn't that be good reason to want people to stay away? *Shoemaker, Shoeman, Sholkin* — his eyes flowed over the list of names — *Sholl, Shore, Short*. Perhaps she *had* only dreamt the name, he thought. But suddenly his eyes alighted on *Shoshawna of the Fire Tribe: see Nathaniel Thrush*. Then she *hadn't* made up the name. Kip pulled down the volume marked *T*, checked for the right page, and turned to the Thrush family tree. Beneath *Nathaniel Thrush*, he read *Adopted daughter, Shoshawna*. As he looked at the names, Theo's description of the dream came back to him: "And before she drowned, she set a baby down. I'm almost sure I heard it cry. And the wind called Shoshawna, hush Shoshawna." Kip began to feel uneasy as his eyes traveled down the list of descendants. *Creighton, Stoddard, Priest, Perth, Beech, Krup, Falloway* — not a trace of Indian ancestry reflected in the names of Shoshawna's grandchildren. *Stanton, Blake, Pierce, Cranston, Wheaton . . .* nor were these names Kip had ever heard on the island. It didn't seem he would find his answer here, he was thinking when his eyes stopped dead, frozen on the last three names on the page. Elise

Tourain, a direct descendant of Shoshawna, was the first wife of William Benedict. Beneath these two names the last entry in Shoshawna's line read *Theda Benedict*.

A picture began to form in Kip's mind. Could Theo have heard about her island ancestor and forgotten? Possibly, Kip thought, and then he moved on. Theo's pendant bore the mark of the manito of her ancestor. If the Amontis were descended from the Earth tribe, then why would they give her a gift with the mark of the Fire tribe, unless they knew?

Kip walked back through the archway. The woman seated at the information desk was still busy with the tour group. Outside, the street had grown quiet and the sun felt hotter. It beat furiously down, in places even melting the tar, which stuck to the wheels of Kip's bike as he pedaled through town. The tourists, all quieter than usual and more sluggish with the heat, crowded together in the shade of restaurants, shops, and bars. The white sand on the abandoned beaches was unbearably hot. The heat wave over the island was building as the solstice approached.

Theo and her father arrived at the Historical Society soon after Kip left. Over breakfast in town, they'd mapped out a tour of the island for their last full day. The Society was one of the places they had agreed upon. Afterward, they planned to charter a boat for an excursion around the island.

"Don't you want to look at the whaling exhibit?" Mr. Benedict asked when Theo headed past the empty reception area toward the reading room. Throughout the past five hours of sightseeing with her father, Theo had anxiously awaited this chance to find out more about Shoshawna.

"I . . . I wanted to look something up."

"What's that?" he asked.

"A name I heard," Theo answered. "The name of someone who might have lived on the island."

As if from nowhere, Miss Pocket suddenly appeared beneath the archway into the library. "Hello, Mr. Benedict." She stretched out her hand. "I see you took my advice. Are you enjoying the exhibits?"

"We just arrived." Mr. Benedict shook her hand. "This is my daughter, Theo."

"Weren't you just here a day or two ago?" Miss Pocket sounded a bit vague, but her eyes watched Theo closely.

"I was here with Kip Sheridan," Theo answered, recalling how cool the woman had been.

"You were?" her father interrupted, surprised. "Theo, why didn't you tell me you'd already been here?"

She shrugged. "I wanted to come back, anyway, to look up . . ." Her voice trailed off. All at once the name was gone, as if plucked from her mind.

"Is it something I can help you with?" Miss Pocket offered, her gray eyes probing Theo's troubled face.

"I . . . can't remember now." Theo frowned. Miss Pocket's stare was making it hard to concentrate.

"If it comes back to you, just let me know," Miss Pocket said amiably, then turned her attention back to Theo's father. Mr. Benedict told her they planned to finish the day by chartering a fishing boat. Miss Pocket suggested they see Harry Carp, who would give them a very good rate. Then she gave them a personal tour of all the exhibits. Mr. Benedict seemed to enjoy it, but Theo scarcely noticed a thing. Her listless mood continued until she and her father said goodbye to Miss Pocket and headed for the wharves.

Theo sat in the bow of Harry Carp's boat as it chugged past Great Point. The bearlike, whiskered man and her father were fishing with a trawl in the stern. The engine noise pouring up from the hatch drowned out their voices behind her. Seagulls circled the wake, and several sailboats dotted the horizon. This boat trip was exactly the sort of thing that ordinarily would have thrilled Theo. But the open sea now made her strangely uneasy. She stared down at where the bow sliced through the water, watching the water bubble around a reflection of clouds and sky. Spray shot up in her face when the waves slapped the hull, trailing foam like lacy white wings spreading beneath the bow.

A bit of the salty spray stung Theo's eyes. After wiping them with her sleeve, she noticed that a shadow had fallen around her. It made the water black as oil and blotted out the sun. Glancing up, Theo saw a towering wall of water. It wavered like a curtain and advanced with a rushing sound. Her breath caught, she blinked, and then the vision was gone.

Her heart pounding, Theo crawled down to the deck and walked back to the stern.

"Having a good time?" her father asked. Then he

saw she was shivering and her lips were blue.

"I'm . . . cold." She moved unsteadily to the seat and sat beside him. "Can we go back?"

Mr. Benedict wrapped an arm around her and glanced at Harry Carp.

"Forgot you two weren't dressed for this. It gets windy out here in the open." Harry went up to the cabin to turn the boat back around.

"We'll stop at one of those restaurants on the wharf and get a big bowl of chowder," her father said as he briskly rubbed her back and shoulders. "That'll warm you up."

"Dad" — Theo's voice sounded tentative, hoarse — "did it seem to get dark to you . . . just before I came back?"

"Dark? No, why?"

"Nothing." Theo's lower lip trembled as she snuggled under his arm. "I . . . I just thought it got darker."

"You O.K.?" Her father looked at her closely. Theo nodded. He squeezed her. "Here, put on my jacket. I don't want you catching a cold."

Shivering, she slipped his coat over her shoulders. Hang on, Theo, she said to herself. Remember, you're leaving tomorrow. If only I can hold out till then, she thought, maybe the visions will end. Her father continued to massage her shoulders. But nothing would drive away the chill of fear that was growing inside.

"But it just rose to a reading of two on the Richter scale." Mr. Sheridan gripped the phone tightly, trying to control his anger.

"Patience, Sheridan, I'm still working out our plan for mobilization. No one's felt anything yet, so we still have time."

"Whether you feel it yet or not isn't the point, Commander Hardy. It isn't worth the risk to wait and see if this thing blows. I suggest we begin alerting people and issuing some civil defense instructions. If we *do* get a big one, there could be tidal waves. Saul's Hills is the island's highest point. With the delay factor between the foreshocks and any waves resulting from a quake, the Hills are central enough so that just about everyone could make it."

"Saul's Hills. Elevation one hundred and eight. I've just marked it on my map, Sheridan. I'll take it into consideration."

"Consideration!" Kip's father was exasperated. "There's no time for consideration. We should alert the people now and suggest that site. At least we'll be covered in the interim, in the event you haven't come up with a better plan before this thing blows."

"Can you guarantee it's going to blow?"

"You know I can't guarantee anything, Hardy. It's just like sitting on a time bomb and not knowing how great the charge is. But only a fool would sit still and wait to find out. We've *got* to warn the community now. If we wait any longer to act, it may well be too late."

"I'll be the judge of that," the commander said coolly. "Proceed as instructed, restricted code yellow."

"But that's only cautionary level, we can't —"

"Proceed on code yellow," the commander repeated. *"I'm* running this show. Your only responsibility is to watch that damn graph. My men are prepared to move on a second's notice. Don't worry, Sheridan, it's all in hand. Now listen, I just sent a new boy down to relieve you. Go home, Sheridan, get some sleep."

Kip's father still clutched the phone after Hardy hung up. "Who in hell can sleep on a time bomb? Damn you!" he fumed, slamming down the phone.

Kip tried, unsuccessfully, to call Theo several times. When his father came home he finally gave up. He didn't want his father to know he'd disobeyed him and looked up the genealogies. He'd have to wait till morning to talk to Theo.

After supper on the wharf, Mr. Benedict took Theo home. She'd eaten so little that he worried she wasn't feeling well.

"No piano tonight?" he asked as Theo pushed the newspapers to the floor and stretched out on the couch beside him.

"Don't really feel like it." She curled up around one of the pillows.

Her father put down the crossword puzzle and looked at her. "Theo? Will you tell me what's wrong?"

"I'm just tired, Dad." How could she tell him? What could she say? That she'd seen ghosts from the island's past? That she was plagued by nightmares of devastation? What would he think? Anyway, she thought dismally, what could he do to help her? She sensed that wherever the visions came from was not a place her father could touch. But she prayed that when they left the island the nightmares would stay behind.

"Theo, if it's about the divorce . . ."

"It's not, Dad, honest. I'm just tired."

"You know you can tell me if anything's wrong," he persisted.

Theo simply nodded, then they both fell silent.

Whatever's the matter, if she doesn't want to talk I'll have to respect that, he thought. "Want to give me a hand with the crossword?" he asked. "The theme of this one's Ills and Ales. Half of the words are common poisons harmful to man. The rest are brands of beer."

"I don't think I'd be much help," Theo replied distractedly. "I don't really know much about beer."

"I do." Mr. Benedict scrawled something on the paper. "You can do the poisons."

"I don't know much about those, either." Theo wanted just to sit there close to him, not talking, not thinking. She wanted to feel safe from the nightmares and the visions, but even more from the dreaded feeling of what was yet to come.

"Come on." Her father tweaked her toe. "It's easy, look." He showed her the page. "Smoker's poison is nicotine. Cyanide's the poison of spies. I've got strychnine and arsenic already. There's only these few to go." He gave her his pencil. "You take over while I get myself a drink. I couldn't get those four with stars."

Halfheartedly Theo read the first starred clue: *Tuna lovers, beware the dented can.* Her father ought to have gotten that, she thought. Everyone knows it. She began to fill in the tiny boxes. BOTULIS . . . Nope, *botulism* has too many letters. But that's got to be it, she thought to herself. "How do you spell *botulism?*" She looked up at her father, who was standing over the bar.

"Of course. That's the tuna clue, right? But it's the poison, not the disease, so I think the word would be *botulin.*"

Theo tried it. Seven letters; it fit. She went on to the next one, beginning even to enjoy herself. *The deadliest season for salads.* Season, like summer? Theo tried to think of a connection between summer and salads. Vinegar and oil don't go bad, she thought to herself. Some other salad, a summer salad. Potato salad . . . mayonnaise . . . Of course, that's it, the heat and sun of the summer season can turn the seasoning of mayonnaise bad. That's tomain poisoning. She wrote it in. Not enough letters, the spelling was wrong. She was about to ask her father when her eyes locked onto the letters. TOMAIN. She erased and rearranged them. TOMANI, MANTO, MAINTO . . . She continued to stare, closer, her eyes juggling the letters around. Then MANITO, but her eyes kept working, there was something else that these letters spelled. AMITON . . . No, she erased the IT and moved up the ON. AMON . . . AMONTI. The name was an anagram!

"How are you doing?" Her father came back to the couch and sat down.

Theo quickly erased AMONTI and penciled in TO-MAIN. ''Dad, I can't do any more.'' She handed the paper back and started to her feet.

"You're doing O.K., it's just the spelling. *Ptomaine* has a *p* and an *e*. Where are you going?"

"I'm really tired. I think I'll go to bed." Her heart was pounding like a drum, frantic, confused, full of fear. Trying not to run, she moved from the living room down the hall to her bedroom, went through the door and closed it, then stood there, trembling in the dark. The anagram teased her memory, calling back an image of Aron sitting across from her, staring with chameleon eyes. Those eyes, with their knowing look, their shared secret, drew her down through the grayness, through the shadows, to the dark on the other side.

The dark took shape. Theo stood at the end of an alley, damp and steamy with fog. Aron was moving toward her, hunched over. Coming closer he seemed to crouch, then crawl, winding, sliding until he reached her feet. When he coiled, Theo stepped backward. Her footsteps clattered like hooves on the pavement. Looking down, she saw cloven feet where her shoes had been.

18 Summoning the Elements

Miss Pocket stood in the Amontis' living room staring out at the darkness where the fog came rolling in from the shore. Aron sat with his parents, surrounded by other islanders. Most sat or stood quietly. Mr. Hogarth paced. The air in the room felt heavy and damp. The lights flickered as if from some electrical disturbance.

Mr. Hogarth broke the silence. "She shouldn't have found her way to the well on her own. Not this soon. She couldn't have known."

"But she did. She found it and she saw," Miss Pocket said without turning.

"But how?" Mr. Hogarth stopped pacing and frowned.

"She followed the elements. The Wind called her by name."

"Why didn't you stop it?" One of the teachers from Kip's school stared at Miss Pocket's back. She felt his eyes and turned.

"Wind arises from Fire, and Fire controls all. Or have you forgotten?" Her eyes pierced the man. "She's too close, too strong. I can no longer darken these visions alone, or stem the tide of her anger."

"She can't know everything," Mr. Hogarth persisted. "It's too soon, she can't know who we are."

"She may now," Aron said softly. "Last night, when she followed me, I took the shape."

Mr. Hogarth turned on the boy. "You were told not to when she was near. You were told not to stir the elements."

"It couldn't be helped. She sought him out." Aron's mother stood between them.

"The boy's not at fault," Miss Pocket agreed. "And it doesn't help us to argue. There's much to attend to and little time. Her father means to take her away tomorrow. She's on the verge of awakening; afraid. And we have reason to suspect that Hester Sheridan's memory is returning. She will have to be darkened again." Miss Pocket faced the room. "Aron, one of your people must go." The librarian looked at the boy.

"But Adele." Aron's mother crossed the room. "Even if it's true, wouldn't it take time for her to put it all together? And then, who would believe her, after all this time?"

"We can't take the chance. Aron, who of your tribe do you delegate?"

"I'll go," a man volunteered. Aron nodded.

After the man left the room, Miss Pocket turned back to the window. "It will be harder to darken the girl now." She stared out at the thickening fog. "We will have to work together."

"But even if we block her, if she leaves the island before solstice —"

"She will not," Miss Pocket broke in, still watching the fog. "We've waited three centuries for the child to return. Even if we could bring her back again, it would be too late. Marenack will have buried the well by summer's end. The hearts of our people lie in this ground, their blood flows in these waters, and their souls soar in these skies." Miss Pocket turned back toward the room, her gray eyes shining. "This is our land, our home. And for those we hurt in reclaiming it, the innocents, we will grieve. Aron and Michael, stand by your people." The lights in the room grew dim. Clusters of people formed about Aron and Mr. Hogarth. "We will darken her to the mill. Some of her people were imprisoned there once. Those memories, once awakened, will hold her.''

The wail of the island's three foghorns sounded in the distance. Miss Pocket stretched out one arm. ''Norma?'' When her sister was standing by her, Miss Pocket took her hand. The others in the room also joined hands.

At a sign from the raven-haired librarian, Mr. Hogarth closed his eyes and intoned, ''Water, extinguish her flame.'' A small cloud of dense gray moisture took shape in the center of the room. It rose above them till all that was left was a damp mark staining the ceiling.

''Earth, close in darkness around her,'' Aron said softly. A faint hum sounded in the air. Dust filtered down from the beams and the curtains stirred as the tremor shook the floor.

''Wind, guide her to the mill.'' A breeze rose up between Miss Pocket and her sister. Adele Pocket dropped Norma's hand and alone walked out to the terrace and down the steps to the beach. The breeze swirled around her and coasted over the dunes, spinning funnels of sand in its path, shifting and blurring her shadow. Miss Pocket's mind was joined to the wind and shifted with it.

The librarian's legs grew withered and gray, shriveling into twiglike shafts. Where toes had been, black claws grew, connected by fleshy webs. The black skirt billowing above her knees turned ragged with the wind. It fanned out behind her, then fluttered with downy feathers. The feathers crept over her back and her face and sprouted from her shoulders. Her arms stretched above her, flapped down, and unfolded as wings. The flesh of her nose and lips extended and hardened into a beak. Then a deep-throated laugh broke the silence, and the song of the loon soared above the wail of the foghorns.

Sitting at the edge of her bed in the dark, Theo clutched the pendant. Her mind churned with the fragmented images of rooms filled with fire, a hail of glass and brick, and boulders the size of automobiles spat up out of the earth. And surrounding all, looming above like a cobra's hood and blocking out the sky, a great, crushing wall of sea raced furiously toward the island. The trembling in Theo's body filtered down into the earth.

Lost in the terror of these visions, Theo did not hear the rustling wings gliding through her window, or feel the weight of the bird settling behind her on the bed. Standing in her shadow, the loon drew away her fear, darkening Theo's mind with a blank, dreamless sleep. The loon spread its wings, and lifting into the air projected its will into Theo's sleeping form. Like a puppet Theo rose, crossed the room, and climbed through the open window.

Fog smoldered and thickened around her as she walked across the dunes. She treaded through fields, past the marshes and the moors, drawn to the hill above the harbor where long, gray, skeletal arms paddled against the wind, beckoning.

In his sleep Kip kicked the sheets away. Fog crept through his window and over the sill, filling the room with murky, humid air. Downstairs, his mother turned on the fan. His father was speaking on the phone in the hall, sweat beading across his brow.

"One point two? At ten forty-three?" He jotted the numbers down. "Yes, I've got it. Good work, Berger. And call again if you notice anything else."

"Who was it?" Mrs. Sheridan asked as her husband walked back to the kitchen.

"Damn, this heat is intolerable. Feels like it just jumped ten degrees." Mr. Sheridan opened the refrigerator and pulled out a beer.

"Who was it, George? Who called?"

Kip's father sat down. "That fellow I left watching the graphs. He just spotted a little activity. I think —" He cut himself off as a crashing sound came from Gram's room.

Mrs. Sheridan rushed ahead of him down the hall and opened the door to Gram's room. Gram was pressed into a corner, the table and lamp by her bed overturned. "George, by the window," she called in a hushed voice.

"What?" Her husband picked up the lamp and flicked it on.

"Someone's outside, George. They moved away just as I opened the door."

Mr. Sheridan held the lamp to the window screen and peered out at the dunes. Footprints were tracked through the sand alongside the house.

"It's all right," Mrs. Sheridan comforted Gram. She had one arm over Gram's trembling shoulders.

"Stay here," Mr. Sheridan said softly.

"George, be careful," Mrs. Sheridan whispered after him as he started down the hall.

Kip's father opened the back door quietly and stepped outside. Fog swirled thickly around the house, but there was light enough for him to just make out the tracks running by his feet. Half crouched, he followed them around the side of the house. Beneath Gram's window something glistened in the heel of one print. He picked it out of the sand and looked at it closely. It was a large black scale, faintly translucent. He flicked it back to the sand and followed the tracks toward the front of the house.

As they rounded the corner, the prints seemed to run together, then fade, forming a wavy ridge, as if blurred by the wind. By the porch, the winding ridge turned sharply and vanished beneath the house. Mr. Sheridan was about to turn back when he heard a slight movement from the crawlspace behind the porch stairs.

Mrs. Sheridan stepped out on the porch. "George?" She squinted into the darkness.

"I'm over here." His voice came out of the fog.

Glancing down by the steps she saw him stooped in the sand. "I brought a flashlight." She flicked it on. The beam glowed an eerie, smoldering gray. "Did you see anyone?"

"Hand me the light," her husband said quietly.

"What is it, George?"

"I don't know. There's something under the porch. Must be a cat or raccoon. Nothing bigger than that could squeeze under here."

"But I saw someone." She leaned from the railing and handed him the light.

"Whoever it was must have run off." He swept the

ribbon of light over the sand, then under the stairs. The wavy ridged pattern, speckled with more of the shiny black scales, receded beneath them. Crouching again, he shone the light into the crawlspace. Even here the fog was dense, and the light flattened out against it. Something hissed next to his arm and he jerked the beam to one side. A flat black head with slitted gold eyes wavered sinuously a few inches from his face. Its crimson tongue flickered in the light.

"My God," Mr. Sheridan mumbled, frozen under the serpent's gaze. Then the hinged fangs glistened white in its yawning mouth. Kip's father struck its head with the flashlight, once, twice, then beat at the tail as the serpent slithered away.

"George, what is it?" Mrs. Sheridan started down, then went rigid as she saw the flat black head dart by the foot of the stairs. The length of the reptile's body rippled like a thin black wave, winding quickly across the dunes and vanishing into the fog.

"George!" Mrs. Sheridan rushed down the steps.

"It's O.K., Jinny. I think he was more afraid of me than I was of him." He took a deep breath. "Never saw a blacksnake that big before. Must have been six feet, at least." Mr. Sheridan led her back to the porch.

"What was it doing under the stairs?" Mrs. Sheridan looked back at the winding trail in the sand.

"Maybe it got lost in the fog. Blacksnakes don't usually come down this close to shore."

"What about the prowler, George? Do you think we ought to call the police?"

"Whoever it was is gone now. I don't think it's

anything to worry about.'' He glanced back toward the shore as they started inside. "Strange how warm it is with the fog this thick. Can't even feel the breeze that brought it in.'' But this fog had not come from the ocean. It had swept down from a distant hill.

High above the harborside town, the old mill's sails broke free of their locks. Like skeletal arms they churned the thickening fog. The door beneath them creaked on its rusty hinges as it closed, its heavy bolt sliding shut against the night. Black wings flapped up to the rafters, unsettling dust and ancient cobwebs that sifted down on the barefoot figure standing below.

The memories haunting the mill enclosed Theo like the walls of a prison. In her sleep, she now dreamed of people who had suffered beneath this roof. She felt the binding ropes, the hurtful chains, and the lashing whips, and the anger of her race began to smolder and swell with the fog. While the island smothered beneath the burning aura of the kesarak's wrath, the skeletal sails spun faster, charged by the power asleep within.

19 A Gathering of Power

Mr. Benedict awoke to the persistent ringing of the phone. The clock on the nightstand read twenty to nine when he picked up the receiver.

"Hello?" he mumbled groggily.

"Mr. Benedict? Sorry to call so early. This is Kip. Is Theo up yet?"

"Hold on." He set the phone down and shuffled out to the hall.

"Theo?" He rapped at her door. After a moment with no reply, he pushed it open. The gray fog filtering through the window made the room feel dank and small and terribly empty. Seeing the bed made up, he concluded that Theo had gotten an early start on her last day on the island. He closed the window before picking up the extension phone by her bed.

"She's not here, Kip. But I'll tell her that you called."

"Could you ask her to meet me after school?"

"All right, but we're going to be leaving at six. That won't give you two much time."

"Leaving? Back to New York?" Kip sounded surprised.

"Theo didn't tell you?"

"No. But I haven't seen her since Tuesday."

"Well, I'm sure she'll want to say goodbye. I'll have her get her packing done early so she won't have any problem meeting you."

After hanging up, Mr. Benedict walked out to the deck. The fog hid the shoreline, but Theo's towel and sandals were lying on the deck. She must have gone in for a swim to escape the sweltering heat, he decided.

"Kip, your breakfast's on the table!" his mother called out when he hung up the phone. Coming into the kitchen he saw that Gram was unusually agitated, mumbling incoherently and staring across the room. She hadn't touched her breakfast.

"What's wrong?" Kip asked.

"I don't know," his mother answered. "Someone wandered too close to the house last night, came right up by her window. She's been like this ever since. I'm going to ask Dr. Pierce to come out and take a look at her. Maybe it's the heat." His mother sighed.

"Did you see who it was?" Kip asked.

"No. I thought it might be a prowler, but when your father looked around the house whoever it was was gone."

Kip ate distractedly, watching Gram. It seemed that she was staring at the kitchen pegboard, hung by the door. The board was covered with shipping lists, a calendar, and various notes and reminders.

"Sol is," Gram said several times.

"What's she saying?" Kip asked.

"It sounded like *solace*. I wish I knew what she wanted. She seems so riled."

"Maybe it's got to do with something there" — Kip pointed — "on the pegboard."

"I don't think so, Kip. I can't even make out anything but the calendar."

"Sol is," Gram repeated like a chant.

"Kip, you better get moving. You're going to be late for school."

Kip gathered up his books, went to the door, then paused to glance at the pegboard.

"Go on, Kip, you'll let the flies in. Close the door." His mother prodded from behind. But when he let the door swing shut behind him, he noticed there were no flies on the screen. There were *always* flies on the screen, except when there was a storm. Was a storm coming? Kip wondered. Animals and insects seemed to have a special sense about such things.

Outside, the heavy fog covered the ground. It had a sulfurous, dirty-yellow tinge. It felt mucky, sticky and warm, Kip thought — not cool, as fogs often were. And despite the cover, the heat of the sun seemed stronger than the day before. In the distance, the Sankaty fog-horn moaned. Hadn't been a day fog this thick so long as he could remember, Kip thought.

Walking toward his bike he considered again what Gram had been trying to say. "Sol is," he repeated aloud, tossing his book bag into the basket of his bike.

The air on the island was stagnant, yet above Mill Hill, behind a cloak of gray, the weatherworn arms of the old windmill beat at the fog and the stone mill wheel turned. While Theo slept, her power continued to grow.

At school, Kip studied Aron furtively, feeling that he'd never quite seen him before. Aron's broad, chiseled features, his black hair and earthy-toned skin, all punctuated what Kip now knew. The Amontis had given Theo the kesarak stone for reasons greater than their common ancestry. Otherwise, why would they have kept their past a secret? What had *really* happened to Theo after he lost her in Hidden Forest, he wondered, and why were the Benedicts leaving the island so suddenly?

As Kip walked into the locker room, he was struck

by the utter silence. A few boys were murmuring among themselves, but most of them changed quickly and seemed rather glum. "What's the matter? Coach die?" Kip asked, joking to the boy beside him.

"Sheridan, that's sick," the boy whispered.

"Cool it, Kip," the boy behind him mumbled. "You'll get us all in trouble."

Kip frowned around at the room full of boys silently pulling on gym suits. "Hey, what's *with* all you guys?" he asked loudly. "It feels like a funeral in here."

"Now you've done it." The boy beside him shot him an angry glance.

At the end of the aisle, a long shadow slipped out the door to the coach's office. "I'm in *no* mood . . ." a voice said gruffly, then the coach limped into the room. Kip winced at the sight of the man's battered face. His jaw was swollen and one eye was buried beneath a violet bruise. "I told you I wanted it *quiet!*" the coach shouted. His good eye traveled menacingly over the boys lining the benches. "Sheridan, get into your shorts! Any talk out here and you'll be running laps till the end of class!" The coach threw him a look of such anger that Kip took a step back. Then the man turned and limped back to his office.

"What happened to him?" Kip whispered, quickly yanking off his jeans.

"Wilks thinks he got in a fight with a tourist down at one of the waterfront bars," the boy whispered back. "But the rumor is he's been telling the other teachers he tripped down his stairs."

"What stairs?" Kip asked. "He lives in a one-story house."

"That's why Wilks thinks it was a fight. Those jerks from the mainland are always getting tight and picking fights. Come on, we better cool it." The boy turned away just as the coach limped back into the locker room.

Out on the field, the gray-yellow fog was so thick it made playing ball impossible, so the coach settled on calisthenics. As he patrolled the rows of boys he inhaled deeply, as if the fog was an elixir of clean fresh air. He seemed energized by the bad weather, and for the next forty minutes he shouted out the exercise count like a drill sergeant. Kip found it hard to breathe in the fog, and the endless gray only depressed him. The air felt almost dirty, and it seemed to have a slight odor similar to that of damp ash.

The shower after class merely left Kip feeling clammy, and as he was walking to Miss Feldspar's room the humidity seemed to increase so much that his clothes began to cling to his skin.

Miss Feldspar spent the last period of the day in an emotional discussion of Anne Frank's *Diary*. "Although this was the shortest book you've read this term, it may well be the most significant piece of literature we've shared. It's rich with insights about love, and hope, and perseverance . . ."

Kip's mind began to drift as the discussion wore on. He recalled Gram's chant as he stared out the window. The fog seemed to press up against the glass like dirty fingers. "Sol is," Kip repeated silently, glancing up toward the front of the room. Wasn't sol another word for sun? he thought. His eyes settled on the corner of the board where the date was written. 6-20. Tomorrow would be 6-21. Then suddenly it clicked. Of course, Kip thought. Gram *had* been staring at the calendar. Tomorrow would be the date on her list of symbols. But why was it special? And what *was* "Sol is"? What was Gram trying to tell them?

"These people would rather have died than give up their home." Miss Feldspar raised her voice. "You've heard the expression 'Motherland'? This is literally what their country was to them. It was not just a sentimental attachment to their mills and canals and ancient streets. It ran much deeper than that. These people drew their very lives from the land." Miss Feldspar was unusually passionate in her summary. A slight quaver in her voice drew Kip's mind away from the blackboard and back to her words. ". . . but to have been so passive was a fatal mistake. One can be driven back just so far, and then one must make a choice. To perish, or to fight."

Miss Feldspar's speech sounded like a call to arms, Kip thought to himself. Her expression now seemed so fervent that Kip could almost picture the slight, dark teacher running off to battle, her long black braid flapping behind her. For a moment this image amused him, but the longer it stayed in his mind, the less funny it seemed. Staring at Miss Feldspar, he began to see her in an entirely different light, as though he'd never really looked at her until this very moment. Her strong, angular features, black hair, and earthy complexion seemed suddenly heightened. Then he saw it, the resemblance to Aron. Kip's eyes began to move over the class, toward where Aron sat. What he glimpsed caused him to shiver involuntarily. There were a number of faces like Aron's here, some softer and paler as a result of the crossing of racial lines but all with a suggestion of the same angular features, earthen complexion, and hair the color of night. Is it possible? Kip wondered, watching them and their expressions of earnest attention.

"Mr. Sheridan!" Miss Feldspar's voice summoned him back. The color drained from Kip's face. "I know the period's nearly over and there's just one more day of school, but I wouldn't be up here if I didn't think what I had to say was important. Mind paying attention like the rest of the class?"

Feeling every eye in the room on him, Kip straightened in his seat and stared directly ahead, looking attentive but lost in thoughts of his own.

When the period came to an end, Miss Feldspar neglected her ritual of changing the date and erasing the board. She also didn't bother to wait for the room to empty before leaving. This break in her usual routine increased Kip's unease, though he wasn't sure why. Outside, the fog continued to thicken.

After the schoolyard had emptied, Kip was still waiting by the bike rack for Theo. There was no phone he could use to call and find out if she was on her way, and he was afraid that if he left he might miss her. He had no sense of the passing of time; where the sun was, he could not tell. A dingy yellow glow permeated the fog, as if it were lighted from within.

Two cars were left in the lot: the custodian's old gray Volvo, whose color matched that of the fog so closely it barely seemed to exist, and, beside it, Mr. Hogarth's small black coupe. While the mist played tricks with Kip's eyes, changing the coupe into the shape of a monstrous beetle, then into a crouching bear, he heard footsteps echo across the pavement.

". . . the nimbus comes from the girl, it builds with the alignment." Kip recognized Mr. Hogarth's voice and turned toward it, squinting as the man approached. He wondered what *nimbus* meant and who Mr. Hogarth was talking about.

The principal's rigid gait and bulky form appeared through the mist like an oversized crab. "Adele will remain with her until the awakening. Since the scuffle last night, we thought it best to have you watch Hest— Ho! Who's there?" Mr. Hogarth walked stiffly toward Kip.

"Kipper Sheridan, Mr. Hogarth," Kip called out.

"You better go ahead," the principal said to the other man, who Kip now saw was Mr. Samway, the school custodian.

"What are you doing out here?" The principal sounded angry, Kip thought. Or was it only surprise?

"A friend was supposed to meet me here after school," Kip replied nervously.

"Looks like you've been stood up." The principal glanced around, his tone becoming easier, less tense. "The building's empty. Mr. Samway just locked up."

"It wasn't one of the school kids," Kip said uneasily, caught between the bike rack and the bulk of the man. He could not stop staring at the man's face; his broad features, his coloring, were so much like the others. Mr. Hogarth began to frown, looking at Kip closely. Kip lowered his eyes self-consciously and focused on the principal's hands. The fingers seemed swollen and crooked, turned in toward the thumbs a bit, like pincers. The skin was slightly gray and smooth as a sea-worn shell. Or was it just the fog that made it look that way? Kip wondered.

Mr. Hogarth stuck his hands in his pockets. "Hmm. Well, your friend may have been dissuaded by all this fog. Not easy to find your way about out here. Maybe you ought to go home and give your friend a call."

With relief Kip watched the principal back away toward his car. "Better keep that bike on the sidewalks," the man called back. "With fog this thick the road's hardly safe for drivers. Watch it, Samway!" He dodged the custodian's car, which was now backing through the lot. "See what I mean?" Hogarth shouted to Kip.

Kip waited for both cars to drive out, then followed on his bike. Perhaps Mr. Hogarth was right, he thought, perhaps Theo had decided not to come. He rode slowly along the sidewalk and up the grade running by Mill Hill. Suddenly he heard a creaking sound above, as if from the old mill. But the sails were locked, he thought, and in any case, there was no breeze.

After a while, he reached the long undeveloped stretch that ran by the moors. Every hundred yards or so, a shadow would loom by the roadside. Marenack signs, he said to himself and pedaled harder, unnerved by the smothering silence of the fog.

"Looks like we got ourselves all worked up over nothing, eh, Sheridan?" The commander spread his hands over the graph paper and grinned.

"I'd hardly call these readings nothing, Commander Hardy."

"Island had a little itch. Just scratched it, that's all. Come on, Sheridan, admit it. Was I right?"

"Just because it's quieted down doesn't mean we're in the clear." Kip's father shifted uncomfortably in his seat in front of the commander's desk. "We've been lucky so far, that's all. This thing could act right up again without any warning at all. Now's the time to alert people, to issue an evacuation procedure."

The commander sat up stiffly in his chair. "I *forbid* you to start any rumors that could jeopardize this community!"

"Rumors? Jeopardize?" Mr. Sheridan's voice was a mixture of indignation, bewilderment, and anger. The man was being totally irrational, he thought. The whole purpose of an alert was to protect the community, not to harm it.

"This information is restricted, and I'm warning you, Sheridan, if I hear you've talked to anyone about this, I'll have you placed under arrest. *I'm* in charge of the welfare of this community, and I'll decide when to act on this matter, if it's warranted." Hardy glared at him. "Am I understood?"

Mr. Sheridan nodded grudgingly. No one in his right

mind would want to hush this up, given the risk factor. Hardy should be doing everything possible to avert the risk to life. There was more to the commander's insistence on secrecy than met the eye, Kip's father thought. He had no doubt it was a cover-up. But why?

"What do you make of this fog, Sheridan?" Hardy's tone suddenly shifted to casual as he turned toward the window facing the harbor. "Looks thick enough to strangle on. You know, the gulls have been careening into the Brant Point Light all day. MacAbee found eight dead right outside the door. All flew straight into the wall. Worst fog I've ever seen."

Without replying, Kip's father gathered up his graphs and started for the door.

"Won't give up, will you, Sheridan?" The commander's sagging face took on a look of disapproval.

"It's my job," Mr. Sheridan replied coolly. "Once a tremor's been recorded, I'm obligated to follow the shift." He heard Hardy sigh heavily behind him as he started down the hall.

"Have you seen Theo?" Kip's mother asked as he came in the door.

"No. She was supposed to meet me after school but she never showed up. Didn't she call?"

"No, but her father did, several times already. He said she's been gone all day. If you have any idea where she is, he wants you to call him."

"All I know is, he was going to tell her to meet me. I haven't even talked to Theo since Tuesday."

"You better call anyway, just to let him know she

wasn't with you. And close that door, Kip, would you?''

Kip glanced back at the screen door. "It *is* closed, Mom.''

"I don't mean the screen door, I meant the outside door. That fog has a peculiar smell, and it seems to bother Gram.''

"Where is Gram?'' Kip asked, pulling the outside door shut.

"I kept her in bed all day. I think she's coming down with something. Dr. Pierce said he couldn't come out till tomorrow, and I didn't want to take any chances.''

Kip passed Gram's open door on his way to the phone. Her breathing sounded a bit labored, and even from the hall Kip could see she was shivering.

Theo's father answered the phone on the first ring.

"It's Kip, Mr. Benedict. My mother said you're looking for Theo.''

"Is she with you?'' the man asked anxiously.

"No, I don't know where she is. I waited at school but she never showed up. Did you tell her I wanted her to meet me?''

"I never got a chance to. She never came back.''

"Do you think she might have gotten lost in the fog?'' Kip asked.

There was a long silence at the other end. "I was sure she'd be with you,'' Mr. Benedict finally mumbled.

"What time is your plane supposed to leave?''

"At six, if the fog lifts. But Theo hasn't even packed. Look, Kip, if she calls or stops by there, would you let me know right away?''

The worry in Mr. Benedict's voice added to Kip's unease. As he hung up, he heard his father's voice from the kitchen, sounding weary.

"Why's the outside door closed? It's sweltering in here."

"The fog, George. It smells odd, like damp ash. Are you all right? You look exhausted."

"A little disagreement with Orin Hardy," Mr. Sheridan replied, selecting an apple from the fruit bowl.

"Who's Orin Hardy?" Kip asked.

"Chief warrant officer at the Coast Guard station," his father answered as he walked up behind Kip's mother, who stood on her toes stretching to return a jar to an upper cabinet. "What's for supper?"

"Nothing." She closed the cabinet door and turned, wrapping her arms around his neck.

"Nothing? Jinny, I haven't eaten since breakfast."

"Good. Because I'm taking you out to dinner." She smiled brightly.

"How come? What's the occasion?"

"Because we both need a break. I'm not letting you walk into that den for a single minute tonight."

"O.K. with me." Her husband pecked her on the cheek.

"Kip, you don't mind keeping an eye on Gram, do you? We'll only be gone for a couple of hours." Then, turning to her husband, she added, "She's a little under the weather, George. I've had her in bed all day. And she still seems a little shaken from last night."

"What's wrong?" Kip's father asked, looking suddenly concerned.

"Probably just a cold. She doesn't have a fever, but if she isn't better in the morning Dr. Pierce said he'd come out. Why don't you look in on her while I change?"

Kip pulled a bowl of potato salad out of the refrigerator and started picking. Where could Theo have gone? he wondered, his unease steadily growing.

A few minutes later his father came back to the kitchen, still juggling the apple in his hand, a preoccupied look in his eye. Kip wanted to ask him about Hogarth, Feldspar, and the kids in his class. Could so many people on the island be descended from Indians? But his father had warned him to leave the subject alone, and he didn't want to make him angry.

Mr. Sheridan tossed the apple back in the bowl and pulled a folded sheet of graph paper out of his jacket pocket.

"What's that?" Kip asked, waving his fork at the paper.

His father sat down across from him. "I've got a little homework tonight, just like you."

"Not me. School's out tomorrow, remember?"

"Hmm?" His father seemed lost in thought. "Oh, sorry, sport, I forgot. I guess you must be feeling pretty good. We ought to be taking you out to supper, to celebrate."

"Who gives you homework, Dad? That colonel?"

"Commander," Kip's father corrected. "Commander Orin Hardy. No, actually I give myself homework."

Kip narrowed his eyes in concentration. "I've heard that name before. That's the name I saw on the sign."

"What sign?" his father asked, looking over the graph.

"The sign in Hidden Forest. I guess he owns it."

His father looked up. "What are you talking about?"

"The No Trespassing sign in Hidden Forest. It said, 'Contact Orin Hardy for Sale Information.' "

"Orin Hardy? Are you sure?" Now Kip had his father's full attention. Kip nodded, watching the furrows form in his father's brow.

Suddenly, Mr. Sheridan stiffened in his seat and twisted his head around. Dust was drifting down from the overhead lamp. The faint *kee-creak* of a cricket in one of the cupboards suddenly stopped. The air buzzed slightly, and then the phone rang.

Looking distracted, Kip's father walked quickly to the hall and picked up the receiver. "Hello?"

"Berger here, Mr. Sheridan. This machine just drew us a picture again."

"What's the reading?" Mr. Sheridan asked worriedly.

"A one point eight."

"All right, Berger. I'll be right down. Just keep watching the graph." Mr. Sheridan hung up, his mind racing. "Honey?" he called through the bedroom door. "Isn't Hidden Forest owned by Helen Corbet?"

"She died in a nursing home on the mainland over two years ago, George."

"What happened to the estate?"

"You remember, don't you? It was sold at public auction. Poor soul didn't have any family to leave it to."

Mr. Sheridan recalled his first visit to Hardy's office, when Marenack had called. Suddenly it all came together in his mind: Marenack buying up every scrap of available land on the island for development; a choice chunk of property overlooking the moors; Hardy's reluctance to issue a warning about the fault. *Of course,* he thought to himself. Hardy's not keeping this quiet to avert a panic, he's only covering up to protect his own interests. Marenack wouldn't be fool enough to develop over a fault, or anywhere on the island if he knew about the quake potential. News of this thing could knock the bottom right out of the tourist industry. Hardy's holding things up till he makes a deal. He wants to unload that land before Marenack finds out.

"George, could you zip me up?" Mrs. Sheridan asked as she stepped into the hall. But her husband had turned away and reached for the phone. "George, who are you calling?"

"Hardy!" he barked into the receiver. "I want to see you in my office in fifteen minutes!" A short pause. "No, it can't wait! I've waited long enough! I'm giving that alert with or without your damn consent!" He slammed down the phone.

"What alert? George, what's going on?"

"I'll be back as soon as I can." Mr. Sheridan kissed her and ran toward the door.

"George, it's about the fault, isn't it?" she asked tensely.

"I'll call you!" he shouted back as the door slammed shut. A moment later, his pickup roared out of the driveway.

Kip's mother shuffled back to the kitchen, glanced disconsolately at Kip, then sank into the seat beside him.

"Where'd Dad go in such a hurry?"

"To his office." Mrs. Sheridan absently brushed a few crumbs from the table, trying to steady her hand.

20 Race Against Time

At five-thirty, Mr. Benedict finally notified the island police that Theo was missing. Other tourists had lost their way in the fog, they told him, particularly along the back island shore where the landmarks were few. Be patient, they said; if she's roaming around outside, she's bound to come to a road or house sooner or later. But now it was later, and the darkening fog that pressed against the windows of the Stanhope house increased his anxiety. He wandered into Theo's room, paused to leaf through a book on her nightstand, then sat on the edge of her bed. He spotted Theo's pendant caught in a fold of her blanket. Where *was* she? he wondered, picking it up and returning to sit by the phone.

Perspiration soaked the front of Hardy's shirt.

"I can't believe this!" Kip's father lashed out at the man in disgust.

"I know how it looks, but believe me, I wasn't keeping this quiet just in my own interest." The commander's voice quavered. "If there'd been a panic —"

"Don't give me that! You were going to risk several thousand lives just to make a fast buck!" Mr. Sheridan shouted. "You're unbelievable!"

The commander lowered his eyes.

"When were you going to pass papers?"

"Next Thursday." The commander wiped the sweat from his brow.

"You were going to make us wait another week to announce this thing?" Mr. Sheridan pushed the graph across his desk, beneath the commander's face. "What if I wasn't the only one to feel this one?"

"What are you going to do?" The commander knotted his fingers.

"Save your lousy neck and do what I should have done a week ago. Issue a warning immediately." Mr. Sheridan turned toward a map on the wall. "Saul's Hills still seems the best site. Even with the fault running close by, it's the highest point on the island. Open ground, no buildings or trees to fall, and high enough to stay dry if there's a wave." Just as he was sticking a pin in the map, a bit of old plaster flaked down from the ceiling. "Oh Christ!" he exclaimed as he darted to the seismograph.

"What's wrong?" Commander Hardy leaned forward in his seat.

"Another tremor. Now it's a two." He threw the man a worried glance, then quickly became angry. "Are you going to just sit there and sulk?"

"What am I supposed to do?" Sweat was pouring from the commander's face.

"Get on the damn phone and wake the boys in your barracks. Have them start organizing civil defense lines. Then call the radio station and have them ready to broadcast a statement. Better call the police, too, and see how many patrol cars are equipped with loudspeakers. That's one way to get the word out fast."

"It's nearly nine o'clock, Sheridan. Can't this wait till morning?"

"No, Hardy, it can't!" Mr. Sheridan glowered at him. "I've told you till I'm blue in the face! This thing is totally unpredictable. There's no way to tell when a stronger quake may hit. Now get on the phone, and while you're dialing, pray!"

The commander nodded, picked up the phone, and kissed Marenack's Island Amusement Park and five hundred thousand dollars goodbye.

"I'm sorry, sir, but unless you can give us a lead, there's not much we can do till the fog lifts. Coast Guard says it's the thickest ever recorded. You're sure she doesn't know anyone else on the island besides the Sheridan boy?"

"The son of our hosts, the Amontis," Mr. Benedict replied. "But I've tried calling them several times. There's no answer."

"It's a lead, anyway. I'll have one of our cars follow the route from the Amontis' back to your place."

"Should I come along?"

"No, the description's adequate, and it's more

important that you stay put in case she comes home or calls. I'll have a talk with the Sheridan boy. I guess that's it. Uh . . . hold on a minute.''

Mr. Benedict heard another voice muffled in the background. Then the man at the switchboard said, ''One more thing, Mr. Benedict. Has your daughter been swimming at all?''

''A couple days ago. Why?''

''Out on the surfside?''

''Yes, right in front of the house.''

''And today? Was she swimming at all today that you know of?''

A feeling of dread like a cold wind rushed through Theo's father. ''I . . . I don't know. She was gone when I got up.''

''Right. I already have that. Sorry.''

''You don't think . . . ?''

''Just a routine question. I'll get back to you as soon as I can.''

Mr. Benedict hung up and stared at the doors to the deck. The sound of the surf rose up from the shore, and farther up the beach the Sankaty foghorn wailed mournfully out of the darkness. Norma Pocket's warning to Theo their very first day on the island floated up from his memory: ''You have to watch the undertow.'' He crossed to the piano and ran a finger over the keys. The sound seemed only to heighten the empty feeling of the house.

Between shouting instructions to the police and guardsmen, Mr. Sheridan tried to call home. He had to get his family away from the shore, but each time he called, the phone was busy.

When the police phoned, Kip was filled with foreboding. They asked him how good a swimmer he thought Theo was, but he couldn't believe her disappearance had anything to do with the sea. There had to be another explanation. Climbing the stairs to his room after talking to the policeman, Kip thought again of the laughter in the forest, and of Theo's odd dream. Once more he had the feeling that something was wrong, terribly wrong. Not just her disappearance, but everything that led up to it: the discovery that Theo was descended from Shoshawna; the pendant with the mark of the kesarak the Amontis had given her; his finding out that the Amontis themselves were descended from one of the island's tribes; the laughter in the forest; and finally, Gram's list of manito symbols, which had turned up just when all these other things were happening.

Kip sat at his desk and stared at the thick blanket of fog outside his window. "Man two," Gram had said repeatedly, all the time trying to say *manito*. And "Sol is" — what was that supposed to mean? he wondered as he unfolded the list of symbols. Again his eyes alighted on the date scrawled in the corner. 6-21. June twenty-first. Tomorrow.

"Sol is," Kip said aloud, looking at the drawing with the kesarak at the center, surrounded by the other three manitos. "The Configuration of Unified Power," Kip recalled reading from the book. That was when the four manitos linked together to use their powers for a common purpose. But they could only do it once a year, when the kesarak's power reached its peak at the summer solsti—— That's *it!* Kip thought excitedly, reaching for the dictionary at the corner of his desk. *Sol is* is *solstice!*

Kip flipped through the pages till he found the definition. "The longest day of the year," he read, "when the North Pole is aligned at its greatest angle toward the sun. Usually occurring on or about June twenty-first." Kip slammed the book closed. *That's* what Gram had been trying to say! Solstice is tomorrow! Kip's head reeled. Could the Amontis be involving Theo in a ritual of some sort? The Configuration couldn't work without the kesarak at the center, and according to the genealogy chart, Theo was the final descendant in the kesarak's line. And her power — her power would be strongest at solstice . . . A snatch of conversation Kip had heard came to mind: "The nimbus comes from the girl, it builds with the alignment." Had Mr. Hogarth meant the alignment of the sun to the earth? Kip wondered. Was Hogarth in on it too?

Kip quickly turned back through the dictionary to look up *nimbus*. "A cloud or atmosphere surrounding a sacred personage . . ." Kip looked anxiously out at the fog. He thought of what Gram's journal had said about manitos, of what his parents had told him about Gram, about the stroke, and about the Darkening. And none of them believed. He now knew why they wanted Theo, but what were they planning to do? Kip pushed back his chair and started downstairs.

From the hall, he could see his mother reading the

paper at the kitchen table. A voice on the radio behind her was speaking, and she turned her head to listen. If he told her what he thought, she would only be angry and impatient. He knew she would tell him that the legend was nonsense. If they hadn't believed Gram, Kip thought, they certainly wouldn't believe him.

Kip quickly pulled the phone by its cord around the corner into the living room. The radio grew louder as his mother turned up the volume. Kip began to dial Mr. Benedict, then stopped. The man would think he was crazy if he started talking about Indian rituals. And then if Theo's father called his parents, he'd really be in for it, and in the end he'd only have wasted more time. If Theo was at the kesarak's position of power, then he could find her just as fast as the police or anyone else, especially in this fog. Faster, even, he thought to himself. After all, he knew the moors almost as well as he knew the back of his hand.

Kip slipped out the door to the porch, then groped his way down the stairs and alongside the house to his bike. The Sankaty foghorn sounded over his footsteps on the gravel drive. Behind him, he heard the muffled ring of the phone. By the time his mother picked it up he was already coasting down the shoreline drive.

The patrol car crept down the narrow drive to the house at the end of Eel Point. Its headlights flattened out to two discs against the fog, illuminating no more than a few feet of ground ahead. The driver had his head out the window, squinting as he passed a long row of parked cars shrouded in mist. He pulled up to the front of the house, left his headlights on, got out, and started up the walk.

The light over the porch was on, and the front door stood wide open. The officer rang the bell, then shouted out. After waiting a few moments in silence, he shouted again, then started inside. Odd, he thought as he walked from room to room. The door is wide open, the lights are all on, and all those cars are parked out front. He stopped by the door to the deck and watched the fog billowing in, swirling about the lamps, hovering over the deck furniture thick as smoke.

As he started back to the hall, something crackled underfoot. Stooping, he found the carpet littered with dozens of thin black scales. Standing up again, he felt a slight trembling in his legs. It passed in seconds but left him feeling all the more uneasy. He made his way back through the fog-filled hallway and down the stairs to the walk, again feeling a faint trembling sensation. He heard the static from the car intercom crackling through the darkness.

"Perry, where the hell are you?" A metallic voice drifted across the yard.

The officer felt his way cautiously back to his car and reached through the window. He pressed a button and spoke into the hand receiver. "Whit?"

"Perry, where you been?"

"I'm out at the Amonti house on Eel Point. Whit, there's something weird going on."

"You're telling me! We just got a call from the Coast Guard station. You're not going to believe this. They think we're about to get hit with an earthquake."

"What?"

"That's what I said. Listen, the captain wants all cruiser PA systems on in ten minutes. He's going to broadcast evacuation procedures. It's already on the radio, but in case folks aren't listening, all our cars gotta cruise with this thing up top volume. Since you're out at Eel Point, you'll cover the roads around Madaket. You find the Benedict girl yet?"

"Hardly started looking."

"Then let it ride for now. This has priority. Better get started."

Officer Perry sucked in his breath, his finger still on the transmitter. "This has gotta be a joke." He laughed nervously, tossing the receiver across the seat and crawling in.

"No joke, baby." The radio crackled. "See you back here or in heaven. Good luck!"

21 The Shapeshifters

The three Nantucket foghorns sounded and the earth on the moors seemed to shiver, triggering in Kip's imagination a picture of giants stepping ashore. He left his bike by the entrance to the moors and groped his way down the path. It would branch in several directions once he passed the bog, he reminded himself. He would have to be careful not to miss the trail to the forest.

* * *

A police cruiser wound its way up the narrow street below Mill Hill, the loudspeaker perched on its roof barking out a recording issued by the Coast Guard. People in the nearby houses scrambled into shoes and darted for their cars. Above them, the arms of the ancient windmill paddled furiously at the windless sky. Suddenly, its grindstones cracked in a shower of sparks and the flailing sails splintered off. The door to the crumbling mill creaked slowly open.

Kip stumbled over the moors, confused and growing more anxious. He should have passed the bog by now, he thought, but he still hadn't heard the frogs. As he peered into the dark, bushes and boulders seemed like wavering specters buried in a ghostly mist that dissolved and shifted the shapes of things. Unwittingly, Kip strayed from the path and lost his way.

"If he does show up, Mr. Benedict, you'll send him right along?" Kip's mother stood before the door to the Stanhope house looking frightened and tired. Behind her, the young recruit Berger sat at the wheel of the Sheridans' pickup. Gram was bundled up beside him, shivering and feverish.

Mr. Benedict stepped out to the stoop beside her. "If he comes, I'll send him." Out of the fog, the Coast Guard recording blared from a passing cruiser. "And you'll get word to me if you see Theo?" Mr. Benedict looked at her searchingly. He'd resolved to wait at the Stanhope house on the outside chance that Theo might have missed the PA announcements and return.

"If I can't, I'll come back for you myself." Mrs. Sheridan grasped his hand, their eyes locking for a moment, echoing each other's fear.

Creaking, hissing, and laughing, they poured down from the burning mill through the marshes. Across the flats of Monomoy they fluttered, crawled, and slid. Theo, daughter of destiny, led them, her nimbus swelling around her, its light illuminating wings and scales, claws and protruding eyes. The pageant of shapeshifters swept over the Shawkemo Hills and onto the moors.

Kip heard the sirens and muted voices swelling in the distance, but then his ears picked up a rustling sound nearby. He pressed himself to the ground and peered through the inky blackness. A faint orange glow began to filter through the fog. As the light drew near, the earth around it seemed to come alive. A river of blackness slithered across the ground, accompanied by a flapping sound like a line of sheets in the wind. As the core of the nimbus passed, it flared like a torch and the air grew warmer. Kip's heart stood still. In the middle of the light he spotted a figure, barely distinguishable through the fog, wending its way down the hill. When Kip stood to follow, his foot struck something yielding that hissed and rustled away. A familiar eerie laughter floated back to him, hypnotic as the Pied Piper's song.

It was nearly eleven when the Sheridans' pickup turned off the paved 'Sconset Road and headed toward the moors.

"Wait, Mr. Berger! Please stop!" Mrs. Sheridan shouted. She pushed open her door just as the young man stepped on the brakes, then scrambled from her seat to the dirt road below. The red frame of a bicycle jutted out between the shrubs.

"It's Kip's!" she called back excitedly. "He must be here!" Then she turned and shouted Kip's name through the swirling fog. Listening, she could just make out the murmur of distant voices. "Maybe he's already up on Saul's Hills with the others," she said hopefully as she climbed back into the truck. "Drive slowly in case he's still on the trail." Berger put the truck in gear and they rattled up the rocky path.

The Institute of Oceanography was in utter chaos. Now that the island had been mobilized and the community was gathering on Saul's Hills, everyone was anxious to leave the vulnerable building by the harbor.

"Come on, George, there's nothing more we can do here!" a man waiting impatiently outside the door called in.

"Where's Hardy?" Mr. Sheridan called back to him.

"He left about twenty minutes ago."

Figures, Mr. Sheridan thought to himself. Hardy *would* be the first to depart the sinking ship.

"Can you ride out with one of the other boys?" Kip's father asked the man.

"Don't need to, George. My car's outside."

"I'd like you to leave it, if there's anyone you can ride out with."

"You're staying?" the man asked.

"The seismograph can't be moved, and I want to watch it a while longer. There's something funny about this thing. It's not acting the way it should."

"But I thought you said it was totally unpredictable."

"It *should* be unpredictable, that's just what's wrong. Ever since that tremor at six, we've had one every half-hour, each time a little stronger and at nearly even increments. There's a pattern to this."

"George, you can't hang on here."

"I'll be all right. After the foreshock I'll still have a few minutes to get to the moors, if a big one's coming."

"In this fog, George? You're crazy not to leave with the rest of us."

"I can't. Don't you see, there's something strange going on here. The strength of the tremors and the intervals between them aren't at all erratic. I don't know how or why, but if the tremors continue like this, I can radio to Saul's Hills just before conditions reach a critical level."

The man in the doorway pulled a set of keys from his pocket. "I just hope you know what you're doing." He tossed the keys onto a table. "Jinny's going to be awful worried till you're up there with the rest of us, you know."

Mr. Sheridan nodded, then the man turned and hurried down the corridor.

Kip was sure he'd seen her; for a moment at the crest of a hill, where the fog had grown thin. Lit up by that eerie light, her face had been strangely pale and expressionless, like the stony mask of the moon. Kip followed, stumbling through the shrubs, then the fog abruptly closed in again and he lost her.

"Theo!" he called, then listened into the darkness. A dull sound like the rumble of thunder came from beneath the ground. For a moment Kip felt unsteady, then the feeling passed and he heard the sound of distant voices. As he started toward them it began to drizzle — a salty, warm rain, like tears.

While Kip moved off toward Saul's Hills, Theo descended the slope to Hidden Forest. The ground shivered like a living thing when she entered the woods. On the ridge behind her the Pocket sisters, the Amontis, Mr. Hogarth, and all the others in shapeshifted forms waited and listened. They could hear the trees bending toward her, guiding her way. The wind rose, and they heard the new kesarak's name whispered through the leaves. Then they turned and divided by element, Mr. Hogarth leading his armored tribe toward Sachacha Pond, Aron gliding ahead of his people toward Harp of the Winds, and the Pocket sisters rising on the wind, soaring off toward Altar Rock.

Behind them, a steady drumlike beating pulsed beneath the forest floor, as the last of the kesaraks approached the heart of the island, the well of her power.

After losing his way a half-dozen times, Kip finally reached Saul's Hills. Drenched to the skin and covered with mud, he searched through the throngs of people. The tremors continued, growing stronger. Car radios blared their warning, and there was talk of help from the mainland; a fleet of fishing and ferry boats was waiting, if only the fog would lift. After wandering through the crush of people for almost an hour, Kip heard his father's voice coming from a radio, full of static. Pushing through the crowd around a cluster of cars, he spotted his mother through the open door of a cruiser.

"Mom!" He ran to her.

Mrs. Sheridan dropped the transmitter in her hand and, starting from her seat, she pulled him toward her. "Kip! I *knew* you'd be here! I *knew* it!" She hugged him tightly. "What happened to you? You're soaking wet. Kip, are you all right?"

"Mom, I felt it! I felt the ground move!" Kip struggled free. "Where's Gram? I have to ask her, she'll know —"

"Why did you leave without telling me?" she interrupted. "Do you know what a panic we've been in?"

"I had to go looking for Theo, Mom. I had a hunch about where she might be."

"Is she *here*?" His mother's look was imploring, expectant.

"I saw her on the moors, down in the valley, then I lost her."

"Thank God she's all right." His mother embraced him again, tears welling in her eyes. Kip's father's voice crackled over the radio and his mother let him go. She grabbed the transmitter and held it with both hands. "Kip's here, George! He just found me! And he said he saw Theo, too!"

"You better let Benedict know right away."

"There's no way to reach him from here, George. Can you call him?"

"The phones are out. That last tremor frightened off whoever was left at the phone company. Better get one of the cruisers to go back down and get him."

"George, when are you coming? We felt something here a few minutes ago."

"There's still time, Jinny. Don't worry about me. Look, you better send someone after Benedict. I'll talk to you when you get back."

Kip set in again when his mother put down the receiver. "Mom, we have to talk to Gram! She knows what's going on, she can help us find Theo."

"Is Theo hurt?"

"I don't think so, but there were snakes and this light all around and I heard —"

"Kip, I've got to find someone to go back for Theo's father," she interrupted. "I left Gram in the truck over there. Do you see it?" She gestured toward the roof of the red pickup on the other side of a crowd of people. "I want you to stay with her until I come back. Then we'll get someone to look for Theo."

Kip nodded, then worked his way back through the crowd. He was anxious to talk to Gram. Mrs. Sheridan watched until he moved out of sight through the people around the pickup, then she spoke to an officer leaning against a cruiser a few yards away. "That man down at the Stanhope house is ready to be picked up. My son spotted his daughter on the moors.''

"Sorry, Mrs. Sheridan,'' the man replied apologetically. "The whole hillside's jammed up with cars, and all of them are empty. There's no way to get through.'' A tremor shook the ground. The crowded hilltop grew silent. Mrs. Sheridan's eyes darted instinctively back toward the pickup where Kip sat with Gram.

"Where are you going?'' the officer called after her as she started down the slope, but she was lost in her own thoughts, pushing her way through the crowd. Someone damn well better have left keys in one of those cars at the bottom, she thought to herself.

While Kip's mother moved through the maze of cars on the hillside, Kip sat restlessly with Gram. She'd become increasingly talkative but her words were still disjointed, the incoherent sounds of someone speaking through fever. Now and then her whole body trembled as if something were being pulled from inside her, then she would sink back in her seat, semiconscious and breathing deeply. After a couple of minutes the gibberish resumed, this time a bit more clearly.

"San . . . sha . . . oh . . . nay mer.''

"Please, Gram. Try,'' Kip pleaded. "Tell me what to do.''

"Nay mer . . . san sha oh . . . caw, call er.''

"Call her?'' Kip leaned right to her ear.

"Stan!" Gram said with great effort. "Sha . . . dow.''

"Stand shadow?" Kip repeated. "Stand shadow. And call her?" he asked.

Gram nodded and sighed deeply, sinking exhaustedly back in her seat.

"Stand shadow and call her," Kip repeated frantically. "Like in the Darkening? Stand in her shadow?"

"Nay mer . . . Name lift dark." Gram trembled uncontrollably, then seemed to lose consciousness.

"Gram!" Kip leaned over her anxiously, stroking the wisps of hair from her brow.

Slowly, she began to breathe deeply again. Without opening her eyes, she said clearly, "Stand in her shadow . . Name her. Call her back." Weakly, she pushed him away. "Go . Name her."

Kip took a flashlight from the glove compartment and crawled down from his seat. He was reluctant to leave Gram alone in this state, and afraid to return to the forest. But he trusted Gram understood the power and purpose of the manitos.

"Name her," he repeated to himself. "Stand in her shadow and call her back."

By 4:40 A.M. the drizzle had turned to a heavy shower, and several tremors of increasing strength had cracked the walls of the house and shattered the doors to the deck. Mr. Benedict stared out at the sheets of rain pouring onto the sand. It pounded down the fog till all that remained was a bleary mist. The sky again was visible, a deep smoky gray that lightened as dawn approached.

A rain-soaked towel was draped on the railing of the deck. Beneath it, Theo's sandals floated in puddles. Beyond them, Mr. Benedict could see the tide moving closer to the house.

Maybe she'd been found and brought to Saul's Hills, he thought, grasping a frayed thread of hope. With thousands of people there, Mrs. Sheridan could have missed her. It would do no good to wait any longer. He went back to his room for a raincoat.

Mrs. Sheridan found an idling car among the vehicles abandoned near the base of the hills. Although its gas tank was nearly empty, she knew it was her only hope of getting to Benedict. As she shifted gears and backed the car down the slope, a tremor jostled it into an adjacent car and the fenders hooked. In her terror, she slammed down the accelerator and ripped the car free.

Mr. Sheridan, at that moment, was running through the corridors of the Institute of Oceanography. The ceiling was crumbling and the walls were caving in. At exactly 4:48, with the sun just below the horizon, a jolt of unexpected magnitude had rocked the building on its foundation. After nearly eleven hours of evenly spaced increments, this new tremor had broken the sequence. Now the fault was behaving as it should, he thought wryly as he raced down the steps to the walk with windows exploding behind him and a shower of jagged glass spattering the pavement. As he ran down the walk, a fire hydrant cracked at the corner and sprayed like a geyser. He scrambled into the car in the lot, started the motor, and pulled out through the entrance gate.

22 Solstice

Still caught in the shadowy world of the Darkening, Theo had not felt the tremors. She had no sense of time or place, or of the world around her. Like a sleeper she stood at the rim of the well, completing the Configuration of Power.

As the glow preceding sunrise began to spread across the sea, she had a vague sense of something pushing inside her, as if her bones were swelling beneath her skin. But her awareness was deep in the realm of memory. She could not see the downy white fur sprouting from her pores, or feel her heels splitting into cloven hooves. She had no impression whatever of the explosion behind her shoulders as the great white wings unfolded and stretched overhead. Her backbone pierced the skin and slid down into the well, where the water rippled around the milky white scales of a serpent's tail. Her nails extended into claws, and a downy muzzle swelled out from the hinges of her jaws. As the first rays of the solstice sun crept into the forest, a plaintive bleat issued from her throat. Still Theo had no clear sense of the changes in and around her; she only felt a deep and sudden grief.

This sadness grew as the solstice sun cast Theo's shadow behind her. The shadow slipped over the well, across the pine needles, and deep into the woods, mingling with the ancient shadows of the forest, shadows of people and times long past, of the island through the ages. Of a time when the whales had blown off shore and their songs had echoed in the harbor. When the only prints on the dunes were left by a race of delicate deer. When the great horned owls hooted at the moon, their golden eyes flashing with the fire of stars. When starlight alone lit the nights.

The history of Theo's homeland sailed before her. First came the Indians in vessels of peace, people whose lives matched the grace of the deer. Then came the vessels of the colonists, and with them a vivid pageant of injustices spanning centuries. Theo's sadness gave way to anger, and the anger drew fuel from the solstice sun, which burned away the darkness. Her motherland, her race, these sacred grounds, were all on the brink of destruction, and the fury of the kesarak raged at this final affront.

The manitos in their positions of power received the kesarak fire, and together they summoned up the elements.

Driven by hurricane winds, the sand and rain ripped through the hole in the roof, stinging Theo's father where they struck his skin. Mr. Benedict pushed past the beam blocking the doorway and went out into the hall, where flames were racing along the sagging ceiling.

A horn blasted outside above the shrieking wind. Mr. Benedict shielded his face with his raincoat and darted beneath the flames and out the front door, where the wind-driven sand swirled blindingly around him.

"Here!" Mrs. Sheridan called from the window of the car. She blew the horn again. "Theo's on the moors! Kip saw her!" she shouted when he ran toward her. As he climbed in beside her, the roof of the Stanhope house collapsed. A thousand tongues of flame licked the wind as the car pulled out of the drive.

The dunes alongside the road shifted with the gales, drawn up in whirling funnels of sand that spattered the windshield like hail. In many places the surface of the road had been broken, heaved up, and swept away. In others it had vanished beneath drifts of sand, and the tires spun till their traction on the shattered pavement made the car lurch. Navigating more from memory than sight, Mrs. Sheridan drove through the lashing sandstorm.

"She's there? You saw her?" Theo's father asked excitedly as the car rocked with the wind. "Is she all right?"

"She was when Kip saw her!" Mrs. Sheridan reached the road running away from the shoreline drive. As they headed inland, the terrain grew more stable, held in place by the roots of shrubs and scrub pine. Mrs. Sheridan pushed the accelerator to the floor, and the car hurtled up to 'Sconset Road.

Kip's mother relaxed her grip on the wheel slightly when the flats of the moors came into view. Then, as they approached the road leading into the moors, the gas ran out and the car spluttered and slowed to a crawl.

"We're not too far! Can't be more than a mile!" Mrs. Sheridan pushed open the door while the car was still rolling. Theo's father jumped out and followed through the blinding torrents of rain. As the fierce wind coming off the hills pushed them back, he reached for her hand.

The paved road from the town to the moors had been blocked by fallen utility poles, forcing Kip's father to approach Saul's Hills from Quaise. The driving wind splattered the windshield with muddy weeds and the dirt road was rocky, but at least the route was more direct. Craning his neck out the window and using his free hand to shield his eyes, he navigated over the trail by Altar Rock.

A high-pitched, maniacal laugh suddenly exploded above the landmark, ripping through the air and shattering the windshield. A spray of glass showered into the car as it swerved out of control, slid down the muddy embankment through the Circle of Power, and rolled onto its roof. Inside the Circle, the earth itself seemed to draw a breath. The hurricane winds rushed back on themselves, and the land sagged down in a sigh. For a moment utter stillness hung over the moors. Kip's father did not feel the final tremor strike.

When the last quake hit, Kip's mother felt certain the earth itself was exploding. Lying by Theo's father, she clung to the ground as it heaved and shook, watching in terror as the land snapped open and shut like a cavernous mouth. A few yards away, a boulder pushed up through the soil like a monstrous mole.

At last the earth grew still. For a moment Kip's mother and Mr. Benedict just lay there squinting through the dust. As the wind died down, they heard a faint and distant roar, a soft dull rush like the sound of the ocean in a seashell. Pushing herself to her knees, Kip's mother saw a glow through the mist and knew that the town was ablaze. But the roar did not come from the harbor, it came from another direction, from the open sea. Glancing back, she saw that the gray horizon seemed to be rising with the sun. Then the roar of the ocean deepened and the sun slipped below a sheer wall of water, a hundred feet high, advancing toward the island.

23 The Shadow Catcher

Nothing could have prepared Kip for what he found in Hidden Forest. Although the sacred land remained unaffected by the quake and was perfect and still, a maelstrom of shrieking shadows swept up around him as he entered the woods.

The shadows were shaped like half-human creatures with tails and wings and claws. They leapt through the air on ghostly hooves, and howled through the trees like the wind. The cry of the kesaraks assailed him, for the path he was treading passed over their bones and the air he breathed was their own.

The rays of the solstice sun plunged through the forest like spears of fire, passing through the leaping shadows in starry explosions that sent these specters writhing in a frenzied dance of light. Kip shielded his eyes and felt his way through the gnarled and twisted trees. When he reached the edge of the clearing, the light was blinding. Kip stumbled around the open space till he spotted a long black shadow cutting through the grass. As his eyes followed the shadow across the field his knees went weak. He stared at the back of a great winged creature towering above the well, a creature of feathers and claws, hooves and scales, that was white as snow.

"Name her," his grandmother's words whispered in his ear. Kip stepped tentatively into the shadow, unable to pull his eyes away from the terrible beauty of the kesarak standing there defiantly before him.

"Call her back," he remembered. Kip started toward the well. A deep warmth swept through the corridor of shadow, and he felt the earth pulse beneath him. A sudden sadness replaced his fear as the kesarak's memory flowed into him.

"Theo!" He called her name, but the wail of her ancestors rose from the earth to drown him out. *"Shoshawna!"* they roared.

"Theo!" he shouted again. He felt something gently probe his mind. He called again, this time holding fast to the memory of what she was. He felt her name run out of him toward the well like a current. The kesarak shifted, flapping her wings, her tail flicking over the grass. Again he pressed his mind forward. Theo. Theda. The kesarak glanced over her shoulder, and her shape began to shift. The downy muzzle began receding, drawing back into itself. The claws retracted and the wings folded into shoulders. The mournful eyes glancing back at him uncertainly were those of his friend.

A hush fell over Saul's Hills. The shadow of the towering wave seeped like a stain across the shoreline. Foam swirled at the crest as it drew itself higher. Its shadow crossed over the flatlands, onto the moors, up to the foot of the hills. A pair of figures were scrambling up the slope.

The wave leapt across the sky like a vast green net cast out to catch the earth. Then the sky itself seemed to cave in and the world beneath Saul's Hills turned murky and cold.

24 A Memory

"I'm fine, dear. Just a little bit rusty. Like the Tin Man from *The Wizard of Oz*." Kip's grandmother was speaking on a phone in the room of a mainland hotel. "Now don't you worry. That doctor checked me over from head to toe." She glanced at Kip, who was sitting by the window, and winked. "He said the stroke was a misdiagnosis . . . It's a transient form of aphasia . . . What caused it? How would I know? I don't even know how to pronounce half these things . . . I just wish these young doctors would admit it when they don't understand . . . Yes, I'll be careful. Now don't you worry. Just rest up and let those ribs heal."

After hanging up, Gram crossed the room and sat on the arm of Kip's chair. "George said your mother was going to stay till visiting hours were over. He sounded good, don't you think?"

Kip leaned against Gram's side. "Will you ever tell them, Gram?"

"Why? For what reason? They'd never believe it."

"Doesn't it make you feel funny, having them think you were sick all that time? And before, when you found out what was going on, and they thought you were just acting crazy?"

Gram put an arm around Kip and pulled him close. "It's enough for me that you know."

"Aren't you worried they might Darken you again?"

"But they've no reason to." She looked down at him with her most reassuring smile. "They've accomplished what they set out to do. I'm not a threat anymore."

"I wonder if Theo really can't remember." Kip stared down at the busy street. "I wonder, if she's just saying that because . . . because we're different, now. Maybe she just doesn't want anyone to know."

Gram followed Kip's gaze to the street.

"You've seen them change, Gram." Kip turned to face her. "Do you think it could happen without her knowing?"

"I don't know, dear. They're not like us. There's a lot I still don't understand."

"But the Naming. You told me how to bring her back."

"Yes," she said with a smile "But I'd only read about it, in DuLac's journals."

Kip frowned and turned back to the window. There was so much he still wanted to know. "Did Mom tell you she doesn't want us to go back to the island? She said we're going to live somewhere else."

"No. But I didn't expect we would," Gram answered. "There's not much to return to."

"I wonder if anyone will go back," Kip said thoughtfully. "Just about everything was wrecked."

"They'll build it up again, in time."

"The developers, Gram?"

"No, I think those days are past, Kip. Some folks will still visit the island, but not like before."

"Then who do you think will live there?"

"The old families, the ones who always have. Now that it's theirs again." Gram smiled gently down at him, a warm, wrinkled smile. "Weren't you going to meet Theo before she goes back to New York?"

Kip started from his seat. "You know, I keep trying to tell her what happened, what I saw, but she doesn't even want to hear."

"It's better, Kip, if she doesn't remember."

"I guess." Kip hugged his grandmother and started down to the lobby

"I figured I'd find you in here," Mr. Benedict called out as he crossed the hotel's deserted lounge. He grinned at Theo pounding away on the upright piano by the bar. Then, catching the melody, he frowned. "What's wrong?"

"Nothing," she answered, not missing a chord. "Why do you think something's wrong?"

"You're playing Bartók. Bartók always means something's wrong."

"I'm just sorry to leave the island, that's all." Her fingers danced over the polished keys as her father put a hand to her shoulder.

"After all that's happened? I'd think you'd be glad to get home."

"I wish we could stay," Theo said wistfully. "I wish the island was home."

"Still don't remember anything, do you? Theo, there's nothing there."

"The island's still there," Theo said softly, as she neared the end of the piece.

Her father's brows tightened a bit, and for a moment he looked at her closely. "Weren't you going to meet Kip in the lobby to say goodbye?"

"Is it time?" Theo rested her hands on the keys and turned to face him, her eyes a smoky gray in the dimly lit room.

"Just about. Plane leaves in an hour." He searched in his pocket for something. "Almost forgot. I found this when I was getting dressed. Must have picked it up at the Stanhope house." He handed her the pendant. A smile played over Theo's face as she slipped it on. She tucked it under her collar and followed her father out to the lobby.